The Pallbearers of Thanksgiving

by

Milo Savich

Blast Furnace
Chicago, Illinois

The Pallbearers of Thanksgiving © 2023
first appeared in *Steel City, Heavenly Kingdom*, by Milo Savich © 2022.

This is a work of fiction. Names, characters, places and incidents are the products of the author's imagination or are used fictitiously. Any resemblance to actual events, locales, or persons, living or dead, is entirely coincidental, with the exception of Frank Lumpkin, as indicated below, and Thomas Geoghegan.

All rights reserved. No part of this book may be reproduced or utilized in any form or by any means, electronic or mechanical, including photocopying, recording or by any information storage and retrieval system, without permission in writing from the Publisher.

Passages from *Always Bring a Crowd: The Story of Frank Lumpkin, Steelworker*, by Beatrice Lumpkin, reprinted by permission from International Publishers Co., Inc., New York City, © 1999 by Beatrice Lumpkin, appear in *The Pallbearers of Thanksgiving*.

Blast Furnace is an imprint of Unwritten History, Inc.

Inquiries should be addressed to:

Unwritten History, Inc.
P.O. Box 6753
Chicago, IL 60680-6753
e-mail: unwrittenhistory@hotmail.com

ISBN: 978-1-7374709-3-9

Printed in the United States of America

BY THE SAME AUTHOR

Wilde about Holmes (novel)
Steel City, Heavenly Kingdom (stories)

I'll put it to you straight. Get up and fight or lay down and die!

— Frank Lumpkin
*Always Bring a Crowd:
The Story of Frank Lumpkin, Steelworker*

*... everything that changes the world or
breaks our hearts, must always start out from a secret city.*

— Thomas Geoghegan
*Which Side Are You On?
Trying to Be for Labor When It's Flat on Its Back*

The Pallbearers of Thanksgiving

Slanting autumn rains stung the rooftops of South Chicago. Lightning flashed and forked across the morning sky as thunder answered by rattling the windowpanes of the Capri Restaurant, where Mike Lazich and Louie DiAngelo were carrying in a coffin. They did not avail themselves of its bronze handles; instead, Mike held up the rear, while Louie, walking backward, took the lead. Even though the coffin, covered with a pall of clear plastic, was empty, they treated the dark object with all due solemnity. They took short, careful, coordinated steps through the yawning double doors.

— Here? asked Mike, cocking his chin at the long drop-leg table draped in shadow.

— Yeah, over dere.

Together they heaved onto the tabletop the oblong box that old man Kompare had rented to the demonstrators to use as a symbol of their plight. Louie then ambled to the entrance where, by unlatching the great oaken doors, he shut out the trailing wind and rain.

— I wunner if it's gonna stop, said Mike, peeved that his feet were wet because his shoes had let in water.

— I dunno.

Mike shook the rain off his coat and looked around the somber dining room until his eyes returned to the coffin, which now dominated the restaurant with its solemn presence.

— It'd be terrible ta get rained out, said Mike, getting over the queer feeling he had had while driving alone with the oblong box in his van.

Mike's restless fingers folded back the loose plastic covering and found the brass latches, which irrepressible curiosity urged him to release. He flinched as they clicked open, then the upper half of the coffin lid sprang gently upwards like a sullen music box. The muted splendor of the satiny diamond-stitched upholstery within alarmed his eye. The cushioned emptiness was pining for a body. A silent death note ran up and down Mike's spine, then stabbed his gut. It was the same kind of dark brown coffin in which Lazo had been laid to rest. As the grievance man, an elected union official, Mike was obliged to attend all his workers' wakes and extend condolences to the grieving families.

Lazo's widow had said to her boy, who was no more than five: *Tata spava. Vidiš li?*

She lifted the boy by his armpits so that he could see his sleeping tata. The boy, held aloft, grew quiet, and reached to touch his father's coal-fired hands. I knew Lazo back when he was livin' inna boarding house by the mill and savin' up money to bring the missus over from the old country.

The trouble started at Wisconsin when strange midnight explosions began rocking a dilapidated battery of coke ovens that were spitting out high-carbon steel for trucks and farm equipment. Wisconsin clearly wasn't sinking any money back into maintenance, and management wasn't saying anything about it. The steel workers were treading on land quaking from roaring walls of machinery that they had long feared might soon spin out of control and kill them all.

But Death is cunning and strikes at his leisure. Accidents were more common when laborers were sent to do jobs for which they had no training. Bronx, Mike's brother, was the foreman who had sent the four guys, a scarfer, a bar loader, a 5-

by-5 man, and a millwright (who had been demoted to labor so he was just a warm body who could be assigned to any job in the factory) on a routine assignment to clean out the No. 2 blast furnace. Some clown from another crew, who was repairing the dust catcher, turned on the wrong valve, which sent carbon monoxide gas backflowing into the blast furnace shaft. The gas pocket exploded, killing all four laborers: Wally Koza; Pedro Garcia; Jimmy Nolan; and Lazo Babich.

Even though these men had been dead for five years, their ghosts were still haunting the dull gleam of finished steel.

Mike gently closed the lid and let his fingers drumroll familiarly along its top. Lazo has nothing to do with this. Today is about one thing and one thing only: the demonstration. And if the publicity stunt with the coffin works, then we're gonna get our point across and da demonstration'll be a success.

— Coffee? asked Louie from the murky light of the rainshot windows.

Mike turned away from the casket. He felt his spine crack pleasantly.

— Or you wanna beer? Louie asked, his voice lilting as he clicked on the overhead lights.

— Coffee, answered Mike to the gurgling of the pot. Too early for a beer.

— Comin' right up, said Louie, fetching the cups as his broad pock-marked face came into the light.

— You gotta have a gimmick, Mike elaborated.

— Dat's sumptn' de TV stations'll pick right up on, said Louie, pouring the steaming coffee into white cups whose rim was bordered by a soft green impasto.

— Dis represents de death o' de American steelworker, said Mike, gesturing to the coffin with verve and showmanship.

— Ya gotta have a sign dat sez so. Or else dey might t'ink somebody's really inside, Louie reasonably pointed out as he took a seat and cleared the red and white checkered tablecloth from his knees.

— You're right, winced Mike.

— Any word on Karl Malden? asked Louie.

— Nothin' yet, replied Mike as a twinge of anxiety looped a wet knot into his stomach. But he'll be here. I'm sure.

Mike jerked a smoke out of his pack, and offered one to Louie.

— How does dat work? asked Louie as he accepted the cigarette. Gettin' a movie star to show up.

— It ain't bean bag, said Mike, giving Louie a light, then firing up his own. I called a coupla movie studios, but de phone would ring and ring and ring and nobody'd ever answer. Den I finally lucked out and got dis guy at Warner's publicity department who was from Cleveland. His old man was a retired steelworker, so he tol' me who Malden's agent was. So den I called dis agent in Los Angeles, an' I left a message with 'is secretary about how we need Mr. Malden to show up.

Mike stopped. Long grey coils of smoke unfolded around them. Louie didn't need to know any more than he had to. Mike followed up and learned from the secretary that yes, Mr. Malden had received the message, but had not yet replied. That was when Mike realized he was out of his league, so he turned the matter over to Bobby Brkljacha, a.k.a. Bobby B, the hot-shot alderman plus committeeman who funneled all sorts of deals, legal and otherwise, through his law office. If a steel mill were Satan's chop shop, lopping off fingers, hands and limbs, then Bobby B's law office was Hell's Kitchen, where paralegals prepared finger and toe shepherd's pie, fricasseed shank and leg, and limb stew on which the attorneys gorged. All the workman's comp cases came through Bobby B's office, and they were lucrative. Mike was a steerer who pipelined many an injured man to Bobby B. But things were different then. Bobby B turned his back on the steelworkers after the mill went bust.

Mike attended the first court hearing on the Wisconsin Steel bankruptcy with Frank Lumpkin and Javi Rodriquez. Frank was a former boxer; Javi used to lift weights and did a bit of wrestling. But these *bona fide* hard guys were out of their depth, and they didn't understand what the judge and the lawyers were talking about. A company attorney felt sorry for Frank, so he clued him in: The Progressive Steel Workers Union had not filed a class-action suit in bankruptcy court, so none of the workers' claims had been filed. And since no class-action suit had been filed, each individual former Wisconsin Steel employee then had to fill out a claim form to claim back pay and benefits.

— O, said Frank.

Bobby B, who was supposed to have filed the class action lawsuit on behalf of the workers, didn't even bother to show up to the hearing.

The steel workers were afraid to rock the boat and upset Bobby B's operation because they were afraid of his goons. The PSWU had a tradition of violence, so any malcontent who shot his mouth off was threatened with getting his head busted open with a baseball bat. Yet Mike went along with Frank's idea to start up the Save the Steel Mills Committee because he thought he was safe. Even so, a couple of guys later dropped out because they felt intimidated even though there had been no outright intimidation. These men did not believe in taking any unnecessary chances.

The Save the Steel Mills Committee soon set up an office in Frank's basement. King Peter, Javi, and Frank agreed to publish their phone numbers in the *Steel City Sentinel* so workers could call and find out what was going on. The members of the Committee worked tirelessly to help more than two thousand steel workers fill out and file individual claim forms.

Bobby B had not returned Mike's calls regarding Karl Malden's appearance because he was "out of town." Mike couldn't get a straight answer out of anybody until one day he got Jan Polski on the horn, who said, *Bobby B wants me to tell you that he's working on it. If he got people extra work on* Four Friends, *then he can take care of this. So just sit tight.*

— Did you talk to Malden on the phone? asked Louie in a tone of suspicion mingled with envy.

— Believe me! His voice sounds the same on the phone as it does in the movies, said Mike, cultivating the impression.

— What's he like?

— He's an alright guy. Down to earth.

— Da last time a movie star came out here was James Cagney in 1943, said Louie wistfully. He came ta U.S. Steel in Gary ta sell war bonds. My uncle Tony shook hands with 'im.

— Shit, I was six years old then, said Mike.

> *I'm a Yankee Doodle Dandy,*
> *Yankee Doodle do or die....*

Mike didn't have those craggy good looks that Malden had. Mike knew that he had his own look: Charles Bronson could have played him. Who would play Bronx? Robert DeNiro, a natural. Jan Polski, let's see... that guy from *Deer Hunter*, John Savage; and who do we get to play Gavin?... Richard Pryor of course; King Peter is easy cuz he looks just like Ernest Borgnine; Javi, hm... if Ricardo Mantalban were thirty years younger; Bobby B is easy, that guy from *Blue Collar*, Harvey Keitel, he could do it. That would be some movie.

— Some of da guys thought that a Playboy Bunny or Forrest Tucker would be better.

— Nah, said Mike, holding his ground. Malden's movies with Brando pop up on TV alla time: *Waterfront, Streetcar,* 'n' *One-Eyed Jacks.* Dey're classics. Den Malden played a steelworker in *Skagska.* And *Streets of San Francisco* is a hit TV show. You know, Malden's a Serb, and he even worked in U.S. Steel's Gary Works before he went to New York. He's even got a clause in his contract dat stipulates dat 'is real name, Mladen Sekulovich, gotta be mentioned once in every film he acts in. He's gonna do dis. Ya gotta believe me. He's gonna make da demonstration larger 'n' life, his awestruck voice said, emphasizing his complete respect for a man who did something big in the world, a man who escaped his Serbianness, yet somehow managed to embody it.

— How you organizin' dis demonstration?

— Duh Save da Steel Mills Committee. I'm handlin' the newspaper, radio, and TV, and King Peter, Javi, Gavin, and Jan Polski been on da phone for weeks organizin'. Division o' labor an' alla dat, see? We're all countin' on a big turnout, but it's still fuckin' rainin'! said Mike with sudden exasperation as he glanced at the rain-swept windows.

— Dey payin' you? asked Louie.

— Nah, said Mike, waving his hand. Everything's ridin' on dis demonstration.

— Da guys'll come out, said Louie as he got up to meet the cooks who were now shambling through the door. Dey ain't got nuthin' better ta do.

Mike nodded, then his eyes lingered contemplatively on his coffee cup. The Save the Steel Mills Committee is just a stepping stone while I'm angling behind the scenes for that precinct captain's job. Still keepin' it on the QT. *Lepo sa svima,* as the old man used to say. Organizin' dis demonstration is just an audition for Bobby B. If dere's a good turnout, den I'm gonna be a shoe-in. I'll get some respect like in de old days.

— You know what you gonna say on television? asked Louie, mashing out his cigarette in the ashtray.

— Good question!

What story should I tell? Stories are funny things. Dey grow as wild as weeds, and everyone's got hundreds of 'em: happy endings, sad endings, no endings... 'n' dose dat better never see da light o' day.

— Dey can have a shockin' story about de outright lies Wisconsin forced me to tell da workers! called out Mike as Louie was walking away toward the kitchen.

Wisconsin got hit hard after the No. 2 blast furnace accident, and it just kept going downhill. OSHA inspectors took over the factory and spent a week writing up one dangerous safety violation after another: unsafe electrical wiring, leaking gas lines, utter lack of safety training, records that disappeared. The workers were also regularly breathing air seasoned with lead, cadmium, arsenic, and other toxins along with steel and coal dust. OSHA then shut down the No. 3 coke battery to bring it in line with federal laws, so the company started hemorrhaging even more money. Then a new wave of Clean Air laws fucked them, so Wisconsin had to lay off even more workers.

— *Things are going to get better,* Mike recalled saying in the movie palace of his memory, explaining the big change to the workers. *A new comp'ny, Envirodyne, is gonna buy da mill.*

— *Howz it gonna get better when Harvester's losin' money ham over fist?* Bronx piped up.

King Peter, Gavin, and Jan Polski headed up a knot of miserable DPs, Mexicans, Blacks, hunkies, half breeds, northern European ne'er-do-wells, and three-time losers who had gathered round their grievanceman. Their clothes were dusty rags and patches that made them look like tramps.

— An' Envirodyne's gonna get rid o' every troublemaker dat don't perform.

The men had looked confused, and wondered uneasily who their new master might be, and whether the new master might be worse than the old one. They realized that they too could be bought and sold on the open market — like slaves put up for sale with the plantation. And it was all legal. Being a citizen didn't seem to mean much anymore.

The Capri dining room rematerialized before Mike's eyes. He shook his head slowly. This particular story cast him in an unfavorable light. So, in the end, what would they put on TV? Karl Malden, of course! Mr. Malden pulling up in a limousine, joining the march, speaking to the news cameramen, and the vivid memory of his great movie roles lending gravity and credence to the steelworkers' plight. When Karl Malden looks into the camera in close-up and says right to the audience —

— Don't let these shock troops scare you ... thundered the distorted voice of the tape loop that was radiating from the battered sound truck outside.

Gino, the one-armed bandit arrived! Gino the Jokester, Gino Palomino, Gino from Reno, who had to learn how to write left-handed to sign his checks, who to this day signed his name in gawky block printed letters: Giиo!

— Hey, Gino! greeted Mike.

Gino extended his left hand in a counter-hand shake.

Doesn't Gino want justice? That's what I'll say on television: *We want justice!*

Gino's story was complicated.

— Don't send me dat nigger no more, complained Gino, referring to Fred, a lanky, snaggle-toothed former goofball Blackstone Ranger who was clownish and uncooperative, who liked to call out sick at the last minute on his weekend midnight turns.

He fucks around too much. But Bronx said, *You're stuck with him for the turn.*

Cooperation was essential in the rolling mill. The workers got a bonus if they beat a departmental tonnage quota. Bronx' crew was getting sky-high overtime by working Japanese levels of overtime and never taking any vacation days. Bronx ran a tight ship, so his crew took a grim view of shirkers, goof offs, and slackers. They looked out for one another. Sometimes a reliable guy like Javi would come in so shitfaced that he couldn't stand up. The guys would take care of him, let him sleep it off in the locker room, and they'd do his work; however, if Fred had come to work reeking of scotch or Wild Irish Rose, and then broke his neck, they would have said, *Well, that's life!*

Once, when Gino turned his head away for a beat, a ribbon of steel jammed in one of the rollers. Fred had never seen steel buckle before, so the magical sight of a steel flower blossoming before his eyes hypnotized him. Gino saw the disaster flare on the dark side of his eye faster than his voice could leap from his throat. The slinky ribbon of pinkish white steel sprang off the rolling bed in a cobble, so Gino shoulderblocked Fred out of the way as the buckling band twisted upward, snapped off and shot through the air, a slow-motion firework. The wildly gyrating ribbon of steel seared through Gino's right forearm at the elbow. The smoking limb fell to the ground, where its trembling fingers vainly raked the earth. Blood jetted from the sizzling stump of Gino's arm.

Bronx jacked the belt off his waist and applied a tourniquet. Suddenly, as if conjured by a magician, a bottle of vodka appeared. Gino fainted. Medics arrived. One of them took the forearm and threw it into a plastic bag. The medics trundled Gino away on a stretcher and lodged him quickly into a waiting ambulance that howled out of the parking lot.

— Mikey Mike, said Gino, slapping him on the back. Do you know how to spot the Italian plane?
— No.
— It's the one with hair under its wings.
— Get da fuck outta here! said Mike, laughing and tapping his shoulder.
— Did you hear the one about—
— I'm glad you still got yer ol' sense o' humor, said Mike. But today is about one thing and one thing only: da demonstration. Wisconsin's gonna have to pay us severance, benefits, and vacation days.

Four bartenders next appeared, followed by a couple of high-school kids who hand-trucked great blocks of ice into the restaurant. The kids were awed by the coffin. The bartenders stopped dead in their tracks. Gino also took notice. Everyone thought there was a body inside.

— What the fuck is this? asked one of the kids, a pimply blond Polak with a wicked smile riding on his small chin.

The coffin was working its black magic on all those who had gathered around it, as well as on those who had shunned it.

— Excuse me, fellas, said Mike. Please show your respect. Dis coffin represents *Da Death of de American Steel Worker!*

Then still-living American steelworkers began arriving. They were decked out in corner-tap outfits, tanker jackets, and banlon shirts, while others, who had wives and girlfriends in tow, dressed sharp in Sunday suits and overcoats. Even so, a lot of men arrived in grey or blue work clothes that still smelled of smoke and steel. They picked up on the coffin gimmick and approved of the showmanship.

Here comes Javi.

— *Cinga tu madre*! said Mike in greeting.

— Why wasn't Jesus born in the United States? asked Javi.

— I dunno know. Why?

— God couldn't find three wise men and a virgin!

Mike and Javi laughed it up. Javi grew up in South Deering with Gavin. He tells a great story about how when they were eleven, he and Gavin were playing army, conducting reconnaissance of enemy forces, when they overheard a neighbor say....

Here comes King Peter, wearing the same suit he wore in the old days when he was stumping for Mike in Serb Hall. How did he say it? *Glasay te za MIKE LAZICH!*

King Peter slept with a double-barreled shot gun under his bed just in case the Ustashi tried to ambush him. He also had heavy seniority at Wisconsin: he started off as a first loader, then an assistant roller, then a craneman. In twenty-six years, King Peter learned the whole mill. He spoke good English, so he acted as an ombudsman for the other DPs. He translated, filled out forms, and did tax returns for them, but he never took any money. He merely solicited contributions for his rebel Serbian church that refused to accept Tito, and all he used to ask in return was that the men consider his suggestions for support in union elections.

Now King Peter stopped to admire the coffin, the mighty gimmick. He broadly made the sign of a Byzantine cross and said with a sidelong glance of concern:

— Does anyone suspect foul play?

The bystanders laughed, and King Peter laughed along as he joined Mike at the bar.

— So Kompare rented you one after all, said King Peter. I guess he got plenty. Ha!

The funeral parlors sure did have plenty because sometimes four or five guys were dropping dead in a week, guys who were only in their forties or fifties. These undertakers were so busy that they were requisitioning fairy cosmeticians from Northside funeral homes to doll up newly deceased steelworkers before the coffin lid shut for the last time to leave them alone without fire and steel.

King Peter noticed fine lines of anxiety streaking Mike's eyes.

— Don't you worry. We're gonna have a great turnout today, said King Peter.

— You bet we are, said Mike. Lemme buy you a drink.

It was getting close to lunch time, so more people began arriving. A sheepish hand sought out and shook Mike's hand. It was Nefarious Darius. He had left his Mammy in Alabama to get his thrills in the mills. Darius had a round black face with a sympathetic smile. What set him apart was a southern courtliness that Chicago Blacks despised. When he first met Fred, he tol' me, *He don't know a buckeye from a biscuit.*

Darius used to be an earnest laborer until Fred got a hold of him and taught him to play poker, showed him hiding places where he could snooze, and showed him how to cut out early without getting caught. And Fred showed him how to do the absolute minimum amount of work required of him on shitty labor jobs.

— *And don't be actin' country!* Fred used to say, lecturing Darius on how to conduct himself properly at work. *And don't be takin' no shit from* da Man.

Soon Fred had corrupted Darius so thoroughly that he became utterly useless.

Darius was too green to understand that the flow of steel didn't govern the laborers' work. Many of them were Black. They were also the only workers who were subject to the direct orders of the foreman, Bronx, whom they despised.

Fred and Darius used to come to me to file deir grievances at da drop of a hat. And I had to defend 'em each an' every time against Bronx' tryin' ta get 'em ta do some work.

— Thanks for comin', said Mike, knowing that the tables had turned on Darius. We need your support.

— You got it! said Darius.

They laughed and executed an intricate soul handshake that Fred had taught them. The industrial malingerer of old was still hoping to get his old job back.

— I 'member how you used to love crying out: *Barbeque!* recalled Mike. And out came the hot dogs at the end of long sticks dat you guys roasted on salamanders just as Scrubby happened to walk by — just to make Bronx look like shit!

Darius giggled sheepishly.

— Hey, where's Fred? Is he coming?

— You didn't hear about it? Fred, said Darius slowly, lowering his eyes and gesturing futilely with his hand, he be dead.

The news sledgehammered Mike gently.

— I'm very sorry, said Mike. My condolences.

— Thank you.

— How did he die?

— I 'onno. Dey say somebody shot him in a school yard.

— In a school yard?

Mike skillfully segued out of the awkward moment by leading Darius to the buffet where the wives had begun serving hot turkey sandwiches and baked beans. Mike walked slowly back to the bar where he was acting as official greeter. He tried to dispel the image of Fred's limber body bleeding to death in a school yard. What was a grown man doing in a school yard?

Mike was still rather upset with himself. Bronx had gotten right up into his face like an umpire and told him: *You can't make steel with garbage.* And he was right. The air was heavy with steel and smoke. Then Fred shoved Bronx, who put up his dukes. *That was how it started*, reflected Mike. *I gave my own brother the shaft for a union that no longer —*

Here comes Jan Polski wearing a stocking cap and a corduroy coat with frog and toggle fasteners that made him look like a high-school senior.

— *Dzien dobry, stara kurva!*

— Yeah, yeah, replied Jan with besieged civility.

He had gone to some college while working the night shift on the weekend as a part-timer, but he had been tight-lipped about it because he didn't want to get a rep as an intellectual or a Communist. Jan was not only cooperative and willing to work, but he was also an overachiever. On midnight turns, if there were no work, Jan would climb up to the catwalk where, like a poet in his ivory tower, he read book after book about the rise and fall of the verdant, forested kingdoms of Europe, and about the birth of the United States, home of the free, land of the....

— I'm buyin' you a drink, said Mike, shaking Jan's hand warmly.

Jan had proved his foresight by giving his two week notice a month before the mill shut down. He jumped to the other side of the fence when he started volunteering in Bobby B's law office, where he was *one o' dose inna know*. Bobby B gave him a sterling recommendation to the University of Chicago, which Bobby B had attended. After Jan graduated, he unexpectedly broke up with his nice Polish girlfriend and went to law school in New York City. Now he was back in town for the holiday and pitching in at Bobby B's office, as he used to do in the old days. People were expecting him to move back.

— Too early for me! said Jan, demonstrating his prudence as he surveyed the crowd. Bobby B here yet?

— Not yet.

— You mean he's still working on his golf game in Florida, smirked Jan.

— Now dat you mention it, what's goin' on wi' dat precin't cap'n's job? asked Mike suavely out of the side of his mouth.

— O, you haven't heard the big news?

— No, what? drygulped Mike.

— I'm just helping out for a few days. I'm going back to New York on Monday.

— Fer what? asked Mike, who thought Jan's move might not have been so smart.

— I'm clerking for a judge, said Jan airily.

Mike waived him off with feigned disgust as Jan got in line for a hot turkey sandwich.

— As Scrubby used to say, *Fer a Polak, you ain't no dummy!*

Mike surveyed the smelly restaurant. Men were helping themselves to sandwiches, lounging on folding chairs, playing cards, drinking beer. He reckoned thirty percent of the crowd was Black, twenty percent was Mexican, and the rest assorted hunkies. I'm friendly wit' everyone, but honest wit' nobody. I'll tell 'em all dey wanna to hear, and I'll let 'em tell me what to say back, even if I say one thing today and de opposite tomorrow, just like da Mayor does. Dey can go figure it out. *Don't go by what I say, go by what I mean*, sez de Mayor, and he's always one step ahead in da game. Maybe I'm nothin' but a bullshit — Mike laughed out loud in jocose self-recrimination — artist! My job is to cover my own ass by gettin' close to real power — whether it's Scrubby or —

— Hey, Grievanceman, my dick hurts. Write up a grievance for me, will ya? said Bronx who was shaking Mike's hand for the first time in years.

What a relief he's not punching me out.

They had been estranged ever since the plant shut down. Bronx quit high school and then signed up for two tours of duty in Vietnam. Mike was the one who got Bronx into Wisconsin as a laborer. He became in succession a scarfer, a chipper, a millwright, and finally foreman, a company man. *Da No. 3 mill is a piece of cake compared to 'Nam*, Bronx used to say.

Bronx was wearing a squalid army surplus jacket and camouflage pants. His complexion was as dusty and gray as that of a rolling mill mouse, and Mike got a whiff of his baby-fresh scent. Bronx wants Justice, too.

— Hey, your phone ain't workin'. I tried callin' lotsa times, said Mike, as the wet knot in his stomach looped and tightened again.

— Dey cut off my phone twice, replied Bronx, baring his bad teeth. Den de t'ird time, dey wanned a hunerd dollar deposit. Dat's when I figured, aw, fuck it, I don' need no fuckin' telephone. People know where I live.

Acne was rupturing Bronx' face; his eyes drooped; his hair was falling out. Even though the mills had killed something deep inside him, he too wanted his old job back.

— Thanks for showin' up, said Mike with fraternal reconciliation.

— Let's see if one o' dem mau maus tries shootin' me in the parkin' lot, said Bronx, laughing grimly as he angled his way to the bar because there was nowhere else to sit.

And Bronx, as a company man, hated the laborers right back. The inspired verbal abuse that came out of his mouth was repeated far and wide, was often imitated, yet never duplicated. If Fred were juggling ball bearings, then Bronx, his fury ignited, would get in his face and start off: *Hey, you dumb fuckin' nigger!* Fred would lose his rhythm and let the ball bearings fall to the ground. *You t'ink dis is Bozo fuckin' Circus? Can you juggle three ball bearings with one fuckin' finger up your ass, and de other one in your nose?! You coulda gotten yourself killed! Get fuckin' movin', you fuckin' retard*, he would bark. *And pick up dat fuckin' shovel and clean out dat furnace before I turn you into a pound of ubangi sausage, you fuckin' lazy-ass nigger, you!*

Then Fred would defiantly reply:

> I gotta dog,
> His name be Dash.
> I'd rather be a niggah
> 'n dumb white trash!

The uncooperative and useless laborers became virtuous while suffering cruelty at Bronx' hands; meanwhile, Bronx had figured out what each man could take. The Army taught him that.

Bronx, a great egalitarian, next discharged a volley of billingsgate against Ivo, who was supposed to be regulating the temperature of the steel cooking in the furnace. He sometimes overcooked the steel, so the billets got fused together or just plain melted down, and the crew had to drop everything to unclog the oven. Other times, Ivo undercooked the billets, which caused the cold steel to jam up in the roll stands. Bronx had to keep an eye on him. *Hey, Ivo, you fuckin' idiot*, he would casually begin. *Did you learn how to operate a furnace in Auschwitz? Huh, you fuckin' Ustashi piece of shit? What's heavier, a thousand pounds of Jews or a thousand pounds of pig iron? Eh? You fuckin' moron inside-out-Nazi, you!*

Bronx saw the big picture. He forced the men to make something greater than themselves — steel.

The Capri had come back to life, but it was mostly older guys who had nothing else to do, no place else to go. The guys who were under forty had found lower-paying jobs elsewhere or were working a couple of part-time jobs.

Panic tenderly rippled Mike's flesh. Where is Karl Malden going to sit?

— Hey, Louie! Mike hollered, startling him.

— Wha? he replied, the cigarette dangling from his lip, a baton that conducted his speech.

— We need a special table for Mr. Malden, 'n' a real nice lunch, like veal parmesan.

— Don't he eat turkey sandwiches like everybody else? came back Louie, perplexed.

— Is Karl Malden coming? asked a toothless old laborer, his face lighting up.

A stream of new men, whom Mike busily greeted, entered the restaurant. Summoning each one's name from the vaults of memory, he hailed them: Hunkie Joe Potiorek and Cal Thomas, Sam the DP and Tread Mark Miller, Mike the Machinist and Bobby Boom, Cussin' Kevin Connolly and Vito diGiacomo, Nick the Nark and Slow Boat Johnson, Nigger Jim and Hunkie Jim (who joked that they were related), Nickel and Dime Tadeusz and Firecracker Frank Josipovich. Then a big Black head with a two-finger deep Afro surged high above the other workers.

— Icy Mike! said Gavin, appraising his old shop steward's banlon shirt. How far did you chase a niggah to get dat shirt?

He was Jabbin' Gavin, big-headed Gavin, big-hearted Gavin who took a job at Wisconsin after his father died, so he could support his blind mother, his wife, and three children. After four years in the mill, Gavin had proven himself to be reliable to the Hunkies, while at the same time he won the respect of his fellow Blacks. He understood the tension between the streetwise urban brothers and their southern cousins. He could tell the difference between a Polak and a Serb, a Mexican and a Puerto Rican. No one messed with Gavin. He had the roll sets down pat.

But that didn't stop the barrel-chested greasers of Trumbull Park from messing with Gavin. Their favorite pastime was throwing rocks at the cars of Black steel workers who had to drive to work, while poor-ass Blacks who didn't have a car and had to take buses, fared even worse when transferring near the plant. The greasers, who gave vent to the secret desires of their parents, claimed to be fighting against the mongrelization of the White race that would inevitably occur unless the Black invasion were thwarted. One night Gavin, who was the biggest guy in the rolling mill dock, had stopped at a red light at 106th and Torrence Avenue, just a block from Wisconsin's main gate, when some greasers started throwing rocks at his jalopy as they were shouting *Nigger, go home!* A rock smashed his front passenger-side window. Then one greaser had the gall to charge up to the driver's side of Gavin's rustbucket and punch him in the face through the open window. Gavin had had enough. The mob of greasers panicked when six-foot-four Gavin, who was built like Prince Pullins, got out of his car and slammed the door shut. He was ready to rumble. Then a cop showed up out of left field and rescued the greasers. *Get back in your fuckin' car*, said the cop, who didn't arrest anyone. Instead, he just told the greasers to get the fuck out of there. Gavin peeled into the mill parking lot and came stomping into work shouting-mad and pride-hurt because the cop didn't bust any one of those punks.

— *I coulda killed alla dem muthahfuckahs!* fumed Gavin.

King Peter, Javi, and the Hunkie workers apologized to Gavin. Even Hunkies like Ivo Pivo, who were racists, got pissed off because Black steel workers faced the constant threat of violence simply by trying to get to work. Productivity went down and bonuses went out the window. So, King Peter tried to ameliorate the situation by inviting Gavin to visit his home in South Deering, but Gavin declined.

— *I don't want some punk torchin' your garage just cuz I came by for a cup of coffee*, said Gavin.

Then Frank Lumpkin heard about it. Nobody was doing anything to discourage the violence: neither Wisconsin nor the South Deering Improvement Agency (whose motto was *White people gotta control their own communities*), which led Lumpkin to set up an interracial group of steelworkers to stop the harassment of Black steelworkers.

— *They're lockin' the gates at the end of the shift!* called a prankster from the bar, quoting those famous last words.

Then Mike's stomach twisted tighter as those words assaulted his ear and sent shock waves bouncing back and forth off the sheet-metal walls of memory. Now Mike's body shook with the long lost iron building. The roaring machinery used to tell the men what to do. His face blanched as he stared into space. What the machines were really saying back then was *break down, go to pieces, die, disappear.*

Some men were stunned; others laughed hysterically; still others kept a poker face. Some thought they should leave right away; others thought it best to work the whole shift. Then plant security started coming around and telling the workers to take their personal belongings because no one was going to be allowed back in after the gates had been locked.

Then the great walls of machinery in the mill ground to a halt: rolling mills came to a dead stop; blast furnaces powered down; coke ovens cooled. A crane that could have effortlessly seized a man in its serrated jaws, lifted him high in the air, and smashed him to death against the ledges and peaks of machinery, now stood like a tyrannosaurus skeleton, de-animated and ready for the Field Museum. The last billows left the throats of the smokestacks, ascended, and dispersed in the overcast sky. Weird silence reigned.

The men shambled out, casting furtive glances at the mill as it became a mausoleum from which they had to escape before they were entombed within it forever. The subdued steelworkers scattered across the parking lot, but this time no one was horsing around throwing footballs or frisbees, no one was popping open and spraying beer cans; there were no cut-low fights, no hats knocked off, no grab ass. The sullen men got into their rust-buckets and rumbled out of the parking lot for the very last time.

Bitter retrospection assailed Mike. *What a fool I was not to know which way da wind was blowin' after Reagan fucked over dem air traffic controllers.*

— Scrubby's a motherfuckin' moron, shouted Bronx, his mouth spuming. I'd a fragged 'em in 'Nam if I had the chance.

— He's a chithead, said Javi, munching on a turkey sandwich wrapped in silver foil.

Scrubby, the plant manager, was the subject of everlasting memory and universal abuse. He made unreasonable demands on foremen, fired workers on the spot, and treated everyone with open contempt.

A festive carnival spirit now came over the men who had gathered in the Capri. These disposable workers were going to repossess their inalienable rights and get into the ring with the big boss and say, *Fuck you, pal. We're fightin' back!* as they smoked, drank, and swore while dethroning the high and the mighty and elevating the low and the humble.

— Him? Dere's a word for him: a fuckin' hypocrite, said King Peter.

— Scrubby's a lyin'-ass motherfuckin' cracker, said Gavin.

The men held that Scrubby was more than just an ordinary scalawag: he was a low-life douche bag, a two-faced, backstabbing shit-eating idiot, a fucking moron, a turd who stank to high heaven, a piss-drinking devil's apprentice who fucked over the workers, a puke, an ass-wipe, a ... a.... And they did not stop there. They questioned his character and his integrity, his upbringing, his education or lack of it. They presented irrefutable evidence that his mother was a whore and he a whoreson; a congenitally deformed public liar, a sorry excuse for a human being, the Good Lord's aborted first draft, a parasite sucking the blood of the workers: in one word, management.

— If I saw dat cocksucker inna parkin' lot, I'd give him some tire iron therapy! said Bronx, nodding his head vigorously.

The steelworkers readily united and determined that they had to knock some sense into Scrubby, albeit *in absentia*, by beating him with baseball bats, wailing on him with chains, disciplining him with lengths of lead pipe, lashing him with rubber hoses, and administering tire iron therapy to him in privately scheduled sessions. The workers, guided by the notion that the punishment must fit the crime, further determined that Scrubby deserved to be mortified with cold weapons: they stabbed him in the back with a bowie knife, gashed him with a switchblade, poked him with a shiv, stuck him with a stiletto, mangled him with a mace, and jacked him up with a jackknife, slashed him with straight razors, box cutters, and butcher knives; pummeled him with brass knuckles, whacked him with crescent wrenches, attacked him with ball-peen hammers, mallets, sledge hammers, shovels, spades, pitchforks, steel reinforcement rods, car antennae, lengths of plumbing pipe; and when Scrubby went down, they kicked him with steel-toed safety shoes, clodhoppers, Polish gym shoes, Beatle boots. Scrubby, a thoroughly unpleasant and disagreeable individual, deserved to be tied up to a pick-up truck and dragged along Avenue "O" on the S-curve; he deserved to be hung —

— Hanged, corrected Jan Polski. Beef is hung.

Hanged from a tree so that his neck might learn the weight of his ass. Elementary school children would stone his corpse twisting slowly in the lake breeze, and on his chest a passionately handwritten sign served as a moral, a lesson, a warning: *This is what happens when you try to FUCK OVER THE WORKING MAN!*

— But the really sad thing is dat Scrubby ain't missin' no meals, said King Peter. He's sittin' at home with his fam'ly: he eats good, he farts good. He don't give a fuck about us.

— You know, da little guy always gets it inna neck, said Gino, scratching the stump of his arm. We showed up, did dis dangerous fuckin' dirty job, and tried to raise a fam'ly, but da workin' man don't get no fuckin' respect! No fuckin' respect!

— Sadlowski sez guys who coulda been doctors 'n' lawyers who didn't get the right breaks in life ended up workin' inna mill, said Gavin. We got to have some motherfuckin' dignity, too!

— We wuz in a tight spot, said Javi. I wish we wuz in de AFL-CIO. Den at least we'd 'a' had someone lookin' out fer our back.

It was too early for the brutal truth to sink in back then. The mill shut down on a Tuesday. The men didn't know what to do on Wednesday, the next day, or the day after, because the mill had hot-stamped its routines into them. They were ill at ease with their new-found freedom because it quickly soured and frothed into aimlessness and anxiety, because, as they came to realize, they were followers — not leaders. Then Thursday, payday, arrived and the steelworkers got their checks in the mail. The ones who tried to cash their checks at a currency exchange got the bad news first: Wisconsin Steel checks weren't worth the paper they were printed on.

After having been set adrift in the dark, the steel workers started asking questions. Nailed to the cross, they vowed to rise on the third day, and if not on the third day, then on the third week, and if not on the third week, then on the third month, and if not on the third month, then on the third year, and then if not on the third year…. Thus, the steel mills died whispering curses at the roaring world. Eventually, some of the guys began meeting in Frank's basement. His luck ran out a couple of months before the mill shut down when he was chaining up a half-ton bar on the graveyard shift. The cable snapped, and the bar came crashing down on his left foot, which would have been pulped if he hadn't been wearing his safety shoes. Even though his foot was broken in several places, the company doctor wouldn't issue him crutches because the company wanted to keep insurance costs down.

— Management played Black and White and Mexican against each other in all possible combinations to keep us from organizing, said King Peter, as the company's strategy dawned on him in hindsight.

Other things changed their outlook. Frank, they learned, was married to a White woman. The two of them had three sons who did well in school, and the eldest was planning to study law. Javi started coming over to the basement meetings, as did Mike. King Peter started showing up, too, and Gavin. They started making lists of phone numbers of politicians, city and public officials. They divided the labor among themselves, and met on Wednesday nights to share what they had learned over the course of the week. Elected officials gave them the fuller, while government agencies slammed the door in their faces. But slowly the facts began to emerge. This was how the weekly meetings resulted in the birth of the Save the Steel Mills Committee.

— Envirodyne, said Bronx, arching his eyebrow as he lit up.

Jan Polski's ears twitched.

— Bobby B always said Brooks McCormack thought he'd never find a fool big enough to buy the mill, said Jan as he made a vinegar face. What did W.C. Fields say? *I'm gonna take your watch and* —

— Dey say Envirodyne was a coupla guys in blue jeans and college professor who worked out of a garage, scowled Bronx.

— A fuckin' college professor, said King Peter. Вук пojo магарца, as we say in the old country. The fish that swallowed the....

— Anyone who took the time to read *The Times* or *The Trib* could have figured out that Harvester had been outclassed in making construction equipment and trucks, said Jan.

— Who's got time to read? asked Mike. It's a fight and fuck world.

— The company made a spectacularly bad move, Jan calmly continued. Caterpillar was walloping Harvester with bulldozers, and Deere was piledriving them with tractors.

— I thought the shutdown was only going to last a few days, said Mike wistfully, till management and the lawyers and the Wall street types hammered things out.

— Doze fuckin' crooks wuz tryin' to pry concessions from da union before dey let us go back to work, said Bronx indignantly. Dat's what wuz goin' on.

It was, after all, the same old story: strike versus layoff. Which side holds the winning hand? Which side is bluffing? Even so, these rumors were the only roadmap they had to the real world that was hidden within the real world where it was so easy to lose one's way.

— *Don't make no concessions*, said Javi back then, taking a bleaker view. *Just let it fuckin' die.*

— *This ain't no game*, said Jan. *Wisconsin'll never reopen.*

The passage of time effectively undeceived the credulous about what had been done to them right before their very eyes. The workers learned that their medical insurance had been discontinued, and that their supplemental insurance benefits had gone *poof!* too. The Union wasn't going to make any concessions and the company wasn't going to negotiate. Truth, the daughter of Time, had spoken.

— *The jig is up*, said Gino.

The devastating earthquake caused by the collapse of the mill then ramified into thousands of smaller aftershocks, and tens of thousands of after-after-shocks that reverberated throughout Steel City. The shock waves articulated themselves in serially unpaid rent, mortgages, utilities, and subsequent bankruptcies; small businesses were closing and storefronts were going unrented; families were holding garage sales, and they were selling their houses at below-market prices and leaving. Suddenly, the little cash on hand for groceries competed with the little cash on hand for other necessities such as booze and smokes.

— Management sent us a message: *Fuck you, pal. Drop dead!* said Javi

Many of them ended up sleeping the one long night that had to be slept.

— So many steelworkers are dyin' off dat you'd t'ink a war was going on, said Mike.

The old DPs in fedoras and gray work shirts who used to talk on their porches in strange languages on hot summer nights began disappearing imperceptibly. No one was paying union dues, so the PSWU Union Hall fell into disrepair. Soon, all its windows were broken, and the grieving wind plucked plaintive notes from its venetian blinds. Tony Roque, the PSWU president, had vanished. Some people said he flew the friendly skies to Florida; others said he up and died.

Mike realized that Jan was standing next to him, talking to him, expecting an answer.

— Huh?

— You said so many guys are dying off that you'd 'a' thought a war was goin' on, Jan reminded him.

— Oh, yeah, said Mike, floating back to earth.

— And then I said it's common knowledge that these men died because the mills went belly up, said Jan to Bronx, casting a sidelong glance at the coffin. It's called *vicarious responsibility*, but you can't make a case for it stick in court.

More men kept arriving despite the steady rain. The aproned bartenders kept handing out free bottles of *Falstaff*, and the wives of the union activists kept handing out free hot turkey sandwiches. Steelworkers splashed the long drop-leg tables with silver as a half a dozen nickle-and-dime poker games were going on.

Bronx took a seat at the bar next to Jan, who braced himself for the stink of his clothing.

— Please don't hate me because I'm beautiful, joked Bronx in a soap opera voice.

Jan laughed along with the damaged veteran, the rightful heir and successor to Johnny Pepper.

— You read books, continued Bronx, cautiously changing his tone.

— Don't hold it against me! said Jan humorously, drawing swiftly on his cigarette, then smiling out of the corner of his mouth as he exhaled.

— Dere usta be a copy of a book called *Strange but True* in the shitter at Wisconsin, said Bronx, slowly orbiting his theme. Aw, I wish I woulda took it but I didn't t'ink of it when dey closed down da mill. It was a little book dat was filled wit' weird fuckin' tales, true stories dat wuz never more 'n a page long, and dey was about bizarre fucking t'ings dat happened ta real people: a farmer walks into his fields one day and den fuckin' vanishes forever; a ship disappears wit'out trace in da Bermuda Triangle on a sunny day; a man gettin' lifted by a tornado 'n' den gettin' set down a hunerd miles away — uninjured. Dis ain't de sort of shit some beatnik writes in a cold water flat in New York City, makin' it all up as he goes along with a king-sized ashtray, a bottle of booze, and a little marahoojie next to his typewriter — no siree, because it *is strange* but fuckin' *true*, like what's happenin' t' us. We're getting' a lesson dat's all mixed up wit' da death o' steel and da way t'ings are gonna be from now on wit' dat cocksucker Reagan. We're livin' history, the weirdest of all true fuckin' stories, man.

— Those who forget history are condemned to…, replied Jan congenially, echoing Bronx' elaborate sentiment.

An enormous cockroach appeared on the bar. The insect was startled by the noise, so it came to a sudden halt, unsure of where to go. Bronx elbowed Jan. Louie caught sight of the vermin, and brought his palm crashing down, flattening the creature into a brown oval.

— You gotta watch out when dat happens, said Louie, wiping down the counter and washing his hands in the sink.

— He never saw it comin', said Jan, grimacing.

— Shit, said Bronx, dat ain't nuthin'. When I was in 'Nam in '66, we had ants bigger 'n dat fuckin' roach, and when dey bit you, dey raised nasty fuckin' welts. We wuz clearin' a helicopter landin' base inna jungle, and dese fuckin' ants was makin' it impossible to get da job done. We didn't have no fuckin' 'secticide, but we had a fi'ty-fi' gallon drum of dis orange herbicide. Da CO said it would kill anythin' dat moved, so we fuckin' sprayed dat shit all over da place, and da next day dose fuckin' ants — and all da foliage — was gone, said Bronx, dropping his voice a register to make a point.

Jan's eyes glazed as he shook his head in disbelief and hoped to end the conversation, as Bronx turned to see Mike fumbling with an American flag he was trying to drape over the coffin.

— What de fuck *you* tryin' ta do? asked Bronx with exaggerated severity.

— I'm tryin' ta —

— Step aside, civilian, ordered Bronx, rolling off the barstool. Let a soldier do dat.

Mike backed off, leaving the flag hanging in a loose skirt around the coffin.

— Where's Karl Marx? asked Bronx.

— You mean Karl Malden. I'm 'spectin' 'im any minute, said Mike, the knot in his stomach tightening.

— Aw, go by what I mean, not by what I say, muttered Bronx, exhaling a funnel of smoke the color of despair. Ah, fuck. I need safety pins.

The ladies in attendance rooted in their purses and produced the requisite safety pins, which they deposited in a rare unused ashtray. They gathered round to watch Bronx' sure hand fold and dexterously pin the corners of the flag in place, and *voilà*, the blue field of stars took residence in the upper right-hand corner of the coffin.

— Dere we go, said Bronx with evident pride in his handiwork.

— Where'd you learn howta do dat? asked a high school kid.

— Viet fuckin' Nam, son! snapped Bronx. An' I had plenny o' practice.

He raised his hand as if he were going to knock some sense into the kid when a half dozen strangers lugging bulky aluminum carrying cases now surged through the door.

Mike flinched. It's gotta be Karl Malden and his entourage!

A man costumed as an arctic explorer, even though it wasn't that cold outside, led the way. He betrayed his importance with a clipboard. The authoritative figure retracted the fur-lined hood of his parka to reveal his closely cropped, prematurely balding head.

Mike bolted out of his chair and immediately introduced himself to the VIPs.

— I'm Jim Ainsworth, said the man with the clipboard as he surveyed the restaurant. I'm a TV news producer with Channel —.

— Glad you could make it! said Mike with perfect timing, seeking out and shaking Jim's hand vigorously.

They kidded around a bit about the weather, and when Jim's eyes began to wander, Mike advised him to stow the cases along the wall. The crew began unpacking. The steelworkers gaped at the lights, camera, and microphones that emerged to capture, shape, and cut elusive sound and fleeting images — so different from making steel.

— We'll be ready to go in a few minutes, said Jim in a downright upright Harvey's Bristol Cream manner.

— You just tell me what you need, said Mike with complete respect. Anything you need.

The pre-demonstration lunch was taking on its own character and energy. It was focusing the workers' anger, which put color back in their cheeks. The arrival of the news team was validating their rising emotions.

At first, the news team empowered Mike, and the steelworkers conferred new respect on him as they stood in awe of the costly equipment. The camera, in particular, keyed them up as it prepared to memorialize the demonstration for posterity, so those not yet born could see what happened to the steelworkers and how they were fighting back. Yet Mike felt by degrees somehow unkinged as the crew was setting up, because their arrival had quietly altered the balance of power.

The usurpation was so subtle that the steelworkers themselves did not perceive it. They were envious of Mike, who was talking to Jim and his foxy blonde assistant, Jessica. Mike knew how to talk to high-class people, but as Mike spoke to Jim and Jessica, it dawned on him that now nothing was possible without their consent, and he began to grasp that he was out of his league.

— We're expecting Karl Marx any minute, said Mike with comeback, trying to up the ante to let Jim know that he was carrying a strong hand.

Jim shot a quizzical look at Mike.

— I mean Karl Malden, said Mike, correcting his flub.

— That's great, replied Jim. How did you get him?

— I got connections, said Mike mysteriously.

— When's he coming?

— Any minute.

— We'll just start without him. We can pick up shots of Mr. Malden whenever he shows up, said Jim. He'll probably stay only fifteen-twenty minutes anyway.

The casual manner of Jim's reply was, on the one hand, reassuring because Jim was a pro who was going to keep things moving; on the other hand, he treated Mr. Malden's impending arrival as if it were merely a routine celebrity component of the demonstration, as Michael Douglas was for saving dolphins. It therefore occurred to Mike that Jim shared intangible, elusive values with Mr. Malden, as if they belonged to a secret society whose members were elected according to unspoken criteria that they alone needed to understand.

— Jim, you gotta get these guys to tell you their hard luck stories, said Mike with inspiration. Each one 'a dem guys got a moral history to tell. Like Studs Terkel.

Then Jim's unexpressive features took a serious turn, and he looked at Mike as if he were a gunslinger at a showdown.

— What's your hard luck story? asked Jim, shooting from the hip.

— My wife she won't let me see the kids 'cause I haven't been able to send her no money since I lost my job, said Mike, now the guy in the white hat who took a bullet in the heart.

He avoided Jim's eyes and looked instead at his expensive waterproof all-weather boots, while his own feet were coldly squishing in his shoes as he shifted his weight.

— All I do is side jobs, like painting houses, mumbled Mike, lowering his voice as if he were a guy saying his dying words in a movie. I keep fillin' out applications but dey t'row 'em right inna garbage can.

— I see, said Jim, who appeared to be listening closely.

— My wife never worked, see? She was always a housewife. My theory was dat's the place for a woman. Housewife. Take care of da kids and alla dat. She coulda worked. But it wasn't my idea o' livin'. When I came home from da mill I wanted a meal. I never wanted —

— That's enough, said Jim, cutting him short.

The cameraman stopped looking through the eyepiece and unshouldered the camera. The soundman lowered the shotgun mic. They had been shooting all along.

— How did that look? asked Jessica.

The cameraman gave her thumbs up.

— So, I want to start off with something easy and get some shots of the steelworkers inside the restaurant, said Jim. It's still raining.

— No *pro*blem, replied Mike, getting back to business.

— Can we get a shot of you saying something to the steelworkers?

— Frank Lumpkin, said Mike.

— Who?

— Save the Steel Mills, said Mike, reminding him, is organizing dis demo. And Frank —

— I want *you* to say something, said Jim.

— Sure thing! said Mike, not refusing the opportunity that was being handed to him.

Jessica told the cameraman where to stand and how to frame the shot. Then she requested that someone write a sign that read *Death of the American Steelworker* on the coffin. She even produced a big fat black marker. She held up her hands and made an ell seven with her thumb and forefinger that she looked through, and she told Mike where to stand and where to look. A warm light splashed his face, and a surge of energy coursed through his limbs when the cameraman said *rolling*. The steelworkers saw that this was the real McCoy, so they greeted Mike with a vigorous round of applause.

— *We want justice!* cried Mike.

— *We want justice!* the men answered, getting into the spirit.

When the steelworkers saw the cameraman panning in their direction, they lurched forward in their seats to get into the shot.

— And to get justice, continued Mike, we steelworkers gotta get out 'n' demonstrate to protest injustice just like Blacks, just like farm workers, just like da men and women who went out to 116th and Avenue "O" on Memorial Day in 1937.

Mike stepped up to a larger-than-life Mike, and from his pedestal, he stated important, eternal truths the way Karl Malden did when he made that rousing speech in *Waterfront* for the hapless dockworkers. But Mike felt detached, as if he were speaking truth to some elusive, invisible power that might or might not hear his words; that might or might not acknowledge him afterwards. He took a deep breath and pressed on.

— Cut, said Jim. That's great!

Surely there had been a misunderstanding.

— I was just getting started, said Mike, suddenly hurt and perplexed.

— You did great! said Jim with facile praise. The first take is always the best.

He went on to explain that the crew was going to take a lot of shots, then edit them together in the newsroom. In other words, they were going to string together different little snippets of film to make the news story.

— That's how it's done. We're creating an impression, said Jim. We want highlights.

— How much time we gonna get anyway? asked Mike diffidently, wiping the sweat off his brow with a paper napkin.

— That depends on the news editor, replied Jim, checking his mysterious clipboard.

It dawned on Mike that he was no longer an organizer but a kind of petitioner. Perhaps Jim was just a Northside slickeroo, after all, who was now making all sorts of vague promises only to determine at his later convenience which ones would be advantageous to keep.

Mike turned away from the news crew to the window to watch the cubical rain fall on the unreal buildings. No sign of Karl Malden yet. I have to do this or die.

Then sunlight angled through the clouds and smudged the windows with welcome light when Frank Lumpkin barrel-chested his way through the door, his anvil-shaped nose leading the way, followed by his fedora and a grey work shirt. He strode like a bull among a herd of milk cows.

The men gave Frank a standing ovation for the unstinting labor he had invested on behalf of their cause. The cameraman didn't let the moment pass unrecorded.

— Who's he? asked Jim and Jennifer.

Mike patiently reminded them once again who Frank was before he introduced them. Then Jim and Jessica told Frank to stand in the same spot and say something to the steelworkers.

— We're rolling, said the cameraman.

— Let's have a big round of applause for Frank, said Jessica.

Frank nodded in thanks and acknowledgement, and began to speak on the receding tide of applause.

— I want to thank alla you for comin' today, and I want to thank Mike, King Peter, Jan, and Javi for workin' the phones and tellin' everybody about it.

The men began listening to him carefully.

— My idea is to reopen the No. 6 mill, which is brand new, continued Frank. It can function as a mini mill and employ five or six hundred people.

The men applauded and hooted their approval.

— I'll put it to you straight, said Frank. Get up and fight or lay down and die!

— Cut! said Jim. You nailed it, Frank.

Frank, Mike, and Jim agreed that it was a good idea to start the demonstration right away to take advantage of the break in the weather. The card games folded and the men buttoned their coats.

— Where's da pallbearers? I want dat coffin outside, Mike ordered.

The steelworkers rumbled out of Capri's bearing their homemade picket signs.

> *We Want Justice!*
> *We Lost Are Pensions! Whose Gonna Pay?*

and

> *We Ain't Taking Loosing Jobs Laying Down!*

Outside, the fading odors of grime, oil, and iron dust mingled. Broad blades of sunlight hacked through the dirty underbelly of clouds.

Mike felt giddy when Commercial Avenue, a street he had known all his life, became a stage. A police car, flashing its blue light, preceded the demonstrators down the once lively thoroughfare. He took up the chant: *What do we want?* And the steelworkers answered, *We want Justice!*

The camera kept rolling and captured Frank Lumpkin along with Mike and other Save the Steel Mills organizers heading the cortege that bore the flag-draped coffin. The bluish autumn sun nicked gleams off the wet pavement as six steelworkers bore the coffin: King Peter, Gavin, and Gino were on the right, while Jan, Bronx, and Javi were on the left. The cameraman and soundman buzzed around the procession.

Passers-by stopped to watch the solemn procession. A car backfired at a cross-street. The powerful bang sent Bronx diving and leopard crawling beneath a parked pick-up truck. The pallbearers bobbled the oblong box.

— Ya see? It's fake, said one grizzled passer-by.

— Dere ain't nobody inside dat t'ing, laughed a plump woman in brown overcoat.

— Be careful, fellas! Mike cried, his heart leaping into his throat as he noticed the cameraman was filming this, too.

Bronx was cowering beneath the vehicle.

— It's all right, Bronx. It ain't no hand grenade, Gavin said. You can come on out now!

A cold sweat had lacquered Bronx by the time he peeked out from underneath the truck.

— Hey, you crazy fucker, come on! said Javi. Whatsa matter wichoo? Dis ain't no Viet Nam!

— How do you know? asked Bronx as he crawled out from underneath the truck. His clothes were wet. He wiped his mouth with the sleeve of his army jacket, laughed dementedly, and shook his head as he resumed his position as pallbearer.

Mike called out like a drill sergeant: *What do we want?* And the steelworkers answered, *We want Justice!*

Commercial Avenue and its name were now out of tune. Thursday used to be payday, which was also the big shopping night of the week. Thousands of steelworkers and their families converged on the stores that once lined the avenue. Then the bright lights dimmed as Goldblatt's, Fannie May Candies, Big Ben Shoes, Bargain Town, Gassman's, and The Commercial Theater closed one by one and left behind a tatterdemalion thoroughfare of somber old stores and thrift shops that retailed dead men's belongings: second-hand toys, skates, sleds, books no one read, kitchen utensils, used clothing, well-worn hand tools, board games missing pieces, wrist watches that didn't work, hula hoops, ironing boards, bed frames, abraded carpets, coffee makers, mismatched furniture, and scuffed shoes that humbled once-proud display windows and surged onto flimsy drop-leg tables on the sidewalk. But Walgreen's was hanging on for dear life across the street, and Lester's kept on trucking, as did Steel City Furniture, Rene Mendoza's, the Gaiety Theater, and Rewer's Camera farther down the street.

What do we want?
We want Justice!

Impoverished shoppers and curious storekeepers stared first at the coffin, then at the demonstrators. Some shouted occasional words of encouragement or took up the chant for a few rounds.

— If it 'a' been a sunny day, said King Peter, we'd 'a' had five thousand people.

Smoke colored clouds hid the sun, then great billowing sheets of rain began to curtain the steelworkers, who mastered their sullen rage as they swung right and went east on 89th Street. Dago Joe and Gene the Polak, Alabamarama and DP Sam, Harry the Hunkie and Johnny the Mick, Swede Swenson and Mujo Yugo, Jack the Gripper and Speedy Salazar, Slim the Jim and Sam the Slam, Ivo Pivo and Rafe Whitehead, Baldie Bill Brown and Gabby Guzinski, and Hot Shot Dawson and Crazy Jane Crane, Dominic the Dynamo and Khe San Carter, Nefarious Darius, Flim Flam Flannigan, Rubbernose Pete, Tip Top, and Sky High, followed by Hard Guy, Smokey Ray, Smokey Joe, Varvara, Bogie, Chubby Boy, Wagon, Smiley, Bubblenose, Lawyer and wave after wave of men who marched shoulder to shoulder, step for step, shouting in the rain:

What do we want?
We want Justice!

They journeyed slowly through the dilapidated streets of Millgate where the houses had been built before the grading was raised to accommodate the sewer line, so the foundations of these A-frames were ten feet below the sidewalk, where they jammed up against one another like gangland murder victims slumped macabrely against a wall.

The Black residents of Millgate had also taken notice. Instead of viewing this new coalition as progress, they responded with apathy, if not outright irritation and unconcealed mockery. Only fifteen years earlier, Martin Luther King, Jr., had led a far greater number of demonstrators to march just a mile and a half south, on the East Side against housing discrimination and red lining, and they, too, had been trailed by many more news cameramen. Back then, all the White steel workers were against the Black steelworkers who were marching with Dr. King. Management saw to that.

The wind picked up and swept Mike's rainblasted face. He saw allies joining the protest, a hundred guys from U.S. Steel, which had started laying off workers right after Wisconsin closed.

What do we want?
We want Justice!

The U.S. South Works plant was now almost as badly off as Wisconsin. Management had brought the union to its knees by demanding concessions before building a proposed rail mill.

The union grit its teeth and granted the concessions, but the move backfired because it emboldened management to demand even more concessions. Finally, U.S. Steel management humiliated the workers by cancelling the rail mill and, to insult the injured, publicly blamed the union for the collapse.

The rain let up again as the demonstrators reached the gates of U.S. Steel. Jim sent Jessica and the cameraman to set up shots of the speakers who were going to use the make-shift podium on the back of Gino's sound truck, which was festooned with rain-drenched red, white, and blue banners, and an American flag. The pallbearers placed the coffin on two sawhorses right behind the speaker's platform.

Mike was watching the cameraman line up a shot when he realized the camera did not have any Mickey Mouse ears.

— Where does de film go in dat camera? asked Mike, dragging intently on his cigarette as he studied the formidable zoom lens.

— There's no film, the cameraman said, speaking in a Northside accent. It's ENG. It electronically transmits live images to the newsroom downtown. See the transmitter over there? The cameraman nodded in the direction of an antenna projecting from the news crew's white minivan.

— Holy shit!

— It goes straight to video. No more film labs.

Mike twinged. Dis innovation slipped past me. Is film goin' da way of steel? Anyway, it don't really matter if it's film or video or flashcards, just as long as da pitchers get out, da story gets out, da truth gets out.

— You're gonna give your speech from up there? asked the cameraman, rousing Mike from his ruminations.

Mike obliged him by mounting the speaker's platform on the back of the sound truck. His confidence shot straight back up as he surveyed the hundreds of demonstrators. He adjusted the mic stand.

— Testing, testing, one, two, three, said Mike. Can everybody hear me all right?

The crowed pressed forward.

— You think I got a shot at Hollywood? kidded Mike off-mic as the cameraman was framing him.

— You gotta go there and see for yourself, he replied non-judgmentally.

Mike looked on the men bedraggled with rain. He had to speak for these guys who were too disgusted, too foreign, and too stupid to speak for themselves, and he had to present them favorably to their fellow Americans in order to make their grievances heard, their warnings heeded, and their complaints addressed. These men stood in the wind, blinking their eyes with unbelieving astonishment. The wet picket signs had gone bleary and limp in their hands. Even Blacks and Mexicans acquired high cheekbones afflicted by grief and long-suffering eyes that made them look like Serbs or Polaks.

Mike suffered a pang of anticipation that annulled his mental preparation as the demonstrators began to gather 'round the sound truck more closely. When the cameraman said *rolling*, Mike began to speak, overcast sky above him and overcast sky beneath him, as he addressed the train wreck of the steelworkers' lives.

— A steel mill runnin' full blast is da most beautiful sight in da world! began Mike, his voice booming over the loudspeakers. Bronx, fer instance, had a seasoned crew dat didn't even hafta talk. They just knew what to do. Ivo Pivo worked the oven and King Peter loaded the ingots into the rollin' mill. Gavin and de other furnacemen hauled da white-hot billets from de jaws o' da furnace and did deir wizardry, 'n' soon white-hot steel came barrelin' through roll stands at twenty-five miles an hour. Nick, Gino, and Jesus, de operators, babied da white-hot billet back and forth through da roll stands until they rolled out a glowin' ribbon o' steel.

Mike's words, writ large as neon signs, flared over South Chicago in storied walls of sound.

— And you know what? My ol' man didn't want me ta work inna mill. And sure as hell, I don' want my son ta work inna mill. But it's taken for granted: if your ol' man was a millrat, den you're gonna be a millrat too. We put in our time, we lived up to our 'sponsibilities. Now *We want justice*!

— *We want Justice!* chanted the steelworkers, lustily clapping their cold, callused hands. Mike acknowledged their applause, nodded his head sagely, and charged the atmosphere with hope, a hard luck emotion.

— In de ol' days, 'member? My grandfather and other workers grew vegetables on comp'ny property dey wasn't usin' durin' da Depression. My ol' man even grew corn next ta da railroad tracks on 107th just like he did back in de ol' country. We ate tomatoes and cucumbers he grew dere 'n' we was thankful for it too.

The men listened quietly to these memories that Mike had summoned of their ancestors in the land of smoke and steel.

— And you could see it comin', Mike continued. And we kept pertendin' dat nuthin' was happenin'. First da Christmas parties was gone, den da baseball and basketball leagues got de ax, 'n' you could see de busted equipment inna yards and nobody fixin' it. Dey was makin' a buck, all right, but dey didn't put a dime back inna plant. Dey wuz hoodwinkin' us and buyin' yachts and mansions and private jet planes and crap like dat.

The steelworkers booed management. Mike paused until the tide of disapproval had receded.

— I suppose dey had deir own ideas. You know, I had faith inna comp'ny, continued Mike with rueful hindsight. Dey was educated, high-class people dat knew what dey was doin'. I usta tell yous guys, *Don't you worry. Things are lookin' up an' it's clear sailin' ahead*, but boy, did dey play me for a sucker!

The demonstrators grumbled in sullen agreement.

— Uncle Sam's gotta step in to pick up da tab fer our pensions, an' Uncle Sam's gotta keep shellin' out money till da last beneficiary dies. Some people say dis is socialism. I say dat if Chrysler got a big tax break, den dat's socialism too. An' if it's good enough fer 'em, den it's good enough for us!

The demonstrators cheered, whooping up their approval.

— Are we gonna let dose Depression Times come knockin' on our door again? challenged Mike. I say NO! WHAT DO WE WANT?

— *We want justice!* the demonstrators answered, but not in unison and not nearly loud enough.

— *What do we want?* Mike called out again, lending his ear to the rain-soaked demonstrators.

— WE WANT JUSTICE! the men roared back, taking up the chant.

Mike yielded the podium to Joe Francisco, an elderly man who wore glasses. You could see his big-boned body visibly aching with many an injury as he took the mic.

— Down dataway, began Joe, pointing northward, I usta be a caddy at da South Shore Country Club durin' da Depression. It was a big deal to have a millionaire cross my palm with a dime or two for a day's work.

— But it was right here offa 116th and Avenue "O," said Joe, pointing southward now. We was workin' twelve-hour days, seven days a week in 1937, and we was sick of it. My brother went out ta protest on Memorial Day right in fronna Republic, an' I never seen 'im again. Da cops and da Pinkertons gunned 'im and ten other people down dat day in col' blood. Dey was killed, and maybe a hunerd people was wounded.

Joe checked a sob in his throat. There were men and women in the crowd who had been there as children, had seen the police open fire, and had watched the men bleed to death.

The cameraman zoomed in for a choker in anticipation of the moment.

— Durin' da Depression, only poor people lived in Sout' Chicago, said Joe, putting a hard edge on the "ch" in Chicago as only old timers still do. We didn' have no hot runnin' water, and a lotta houses was no better 'n shacks. But da rich lived by da Country Club in fancy houses dat look like museums. Da steel companies want it to be like dat again. It's terrible. It's terrible. And we're not gonna let it happen again, are we? *What do we want?*

WE WANT JUSTICE!

In the old days, Riverview had a freak show that headlined Betty Lou Williams, the four-legged girl, as one of the strangest freaks alive. But today, people flocked to hear Frank Lumpkin, who was next to speak, not because he had four legs, but because he had hope. That made him a one-man freak show.

Frank had the patience of Job with attorneys, who, despite fully agreeing that the steelworkers had gotten stabbed in the back, wouldn't touch the case because it was going to be a decade-long burden with little chance of ever collecting. The unemployed workers didn't even know what a retainer was, much less could they come up with one. At long last, Frank found a young labor lawyer named Tom Geoghegan to take up their cause, and he even managed to convince the partners of his firm to handle the case for which it would defer compensation until a settlement was reached.

When Frank got up on the sound truck, the men suspended their disbelief to hear once again the epic tale of how the workers were going to bring big business to its knees.

— I don't have anything new to tell you, said Frank, but things look good! We, the workers, gotta make things happen. We got our class action lawsuit goin' on behalf of all former PSWU members chargin' that Harvester's sale of the mill to Envirodyne was a fake transaction, and that the agreement Tony Roque signed in 1977 isn't worth the paper it's written on. The lawsuit demands that Harvester pay out benefits to the workers who are entitled to them. The lawyers are right on the case, and they're puttin' time into it every day. They don't get paid until we get paid, so they're clippin' right along as fast as they can. The judge calls the shots. But it's really up to us. We can sit and wait while steel workers die off and don't live to see their money or we can get up and do something, remind people that we still got fight in us, and that we need their support. We can join demonstrations to extend unemployment benefits. Let people see that Wisconsin Steelworkers are supporting them. It won't benefit us directly, but it will benefit other workers. It will benefit our children. We'll join the picket line with our signs. The Save the Steel Mills Committee will be there fightin' for justice!

The men roared like lions and showed their fighting spirit.

— What we've gotta do right now is save Wisconsin's No. 6 mill, the bar mill. Why tear it down? Wisconsin just built it. It's a perfect mini-mill. It can take scrap metal and roll it into bars. Six, seven hundred people could work there.

Frank was the one who thought it up. Everyone thought it was a good idea.

— I went and had meetin's with the mayor, the governor, anyone who'd listen to me, because the Reagan Administration ended up ownin' the mill. This city official sez to me, *What do you want us to do, just hold onto it like a birthday present for next year?* Yeah, I sez. *Oh, so we gotta pay for security guards and all that?* No big deal, I sez. *No can do,* he sez. Nickle and dime madness, money madness. You can't win no argument against money madness. Then he tried to talk me into takin' a job with the Port of Chicago! I didn't want it. *Why?* He asked. *'Cause that's not makin' anything,* I sez. *It's just liftin' and loadin'.*

Frank paused. The men dwelled on the idea of making things. No one could figure out why the government would not want workers to make things.

— We're gonna win our case but we don't know how much money it will be and we don't know how long it's gonna take. We have to take action now, because we'll get a settlement sooner that way. People are freezin' to death because they ain't got money to pay the gas bill. Well, we can picket the gas company till they turn the heat back on. The Wisconsin Steelworkers care about people freezin'. We gotta be out *there* so people know we're *here,* so that people know we're gonna come out on top of this thing. *What do we want?*

The steelworkers waved their signs and chanted defiantly:

WE WANT JUSTICE!

The cameraman was swooping his great lens across the angry faces of the crowd as pandemonium erupted near the news van. Mike's heartbeat tripped, then raced. A limo was pulling up, but Mike was alarmed to see steelworkers, who were brandishing tire irons and baseball bats, surround the luxury automobile. This is absolutely not da way to greet Karl Malden!

Here comes Javi wielding a baseball bat. Here comes Gavin gripping a crowbar. And here comes Bronx with a tire iron that he was tapping gently against the palm of his hand.

Four bodyguards in black suits and wraparound sunglasses emerged from the vehicle. They thrust their arms out, urging the guys to back off.

— Where's our fuckin' pensions! shouted Bronx.

— Yeah, where's our fuckin' pensions? cried others.

When there was no answer, Bronx lunged forward, but King Peter wisely restrained him as the familiar figure's legs scissored out of the limousine.

Bobby B had arrived.

Volley after volley of hoots, catcalls, boos, and curses pommeled Bobby B. The bodyguards, their shoulder holsters bulging in their suit jackets, quickly closed ranks around the professional politician. The bruisers escorted the alderman-committeeman to the sound truck, while the angry steelworkers recoiled as if to make way for a giant sleazy poisonous snake.

The cameraman jostled through the swarming crowd as he tried to get a close-up of Bobby B, but one of the bodyguards shoved him away.

— It's okay, said Bobby B. Let 'im film.

— Get a load of that tan! shouted one heckler.

Threatening Bobby B, no matter how enjoyable a pastime it may have been, was just a warm-up round for the grudge match against Harvester.

Mike descended from the makeshift stage to greet Bobby B and shake his hand, but Frank and Joe and the others avoided him like the plague. Mike was the only one to greet the politician. He extended his hand, smiled, and said:

— Hiya, Bobby!

— This is all your fault! hissed Bobby B through his teeth as he withheld his hand.

Mike froze, stunned by the implication that it was his fault that Bobby B was receiving such a hostile reception.

— But —, began Mike, retracting his rebuffed hand.
— You're gonna pay for this!
— Hey, Bobby! Where's Karl Malden? a heckler bellowed out, so the crowed picked up the line and began chanting
— *Where's Karl Malden?! Where's Karl Malden?!*
Bobby B's bodyguards girdled him more closely. This was not the time for Mike to ask about Karl Malden, nor was it the time to ask why Bobby B hadn't joined the march — much less to ask about the precinct captain's job. Everything started off so well, but now the demonstration was hurtling toward catastrophe.

Alderman-Committeeman Brkljacha took charge of the hectoring crowd. He stripped off his costly Italian suit jacket, rolled up his custom-tailored shirtsleeves, and sprang to the top of the sound truck in a single bound. He used this actorly stunt to hook his audience, who watched with amazement and began to fall under his spell. Bobby B moved with a boxer's bravado up to the mic, but Bronx, who had meanwhile disposed of his tire iron, climbed up on the sound truck under the pretense of straightening out the American flag on the coffin. He grabbed the microphone before Bobby B had a chance to reach it.

— You know what George Washington said? asked Bronx vehemently.

Bobby B didn't know what to say as the demented vet upstaged him. The crowd guffawed and laughed uproariously.

— Wha' did George Washington say, Bobby? cried a heckler.
— What? I don't get it, said Bobby B cautiously.
— You know what George Washington said? Bronx slowly repeated.

Bobby B's stiffness was funnier than Bronx' question.

— He said lotsa stuff, replied Bobby B oleagenously.
— George Washington said *all men are created equal.* He said we gotta *right to life, liberty, and da pursuit of happiness.*

An' he said *don't fuck over da workin' man!* Dat's what he said! So, where's our pensions?

The steel workers roared as Bronx put the mic back on its stand and leapt off the truck back into the swelling crowd.

— *Where's our pensions?* chanted the demonstrators, inspired by Bronx' stunt.

Mike's heart sank. Bronx had put the nail in his coffin.

Bobby B, however, had nowhere to go but up. His poise said he was standing up for Justice, and he was suggesting that he could straighten out big problems with small words, fell a giant with a single stone, and yes, even reopen the mill. He grasped a roll bar on the sound truck above his head and jousted his torso into the boisterous crowd of angry men whose wives were pissed off, whose children were hungry, and whose mortgages were defaulting. Bobby B bowed his head and raised his hand to request a pause. Then he lifted his face to the crowd with wearisome resolution when the roar of disapproval had abated.

— I've been talkin' to everyone, includin' da mayor and the gov'nor, he said, his powerful voice drowning out lingering hecklers.

Bobby B jabbed the chest of his absent opponent, so everyone knew the empty air contained vampires who were sucking their blood: the businessmen, the board of directors, the bankers, the lawyers, and the politicians, all of whom had made a shit pot of money off the workers, and who then cut them loose once they couldn't make any more money off them.

— I wanna see da mill up and runnin' as soon as poss'ble and getcha da money you got comin' to you....

The steelworkers reluctantly permitted the man in the Italian suit to make his point.

— It was play money, said Bobby B. Stock transfers and options. It was just smoke and mirrors. Envirodyne didn't have a plug nickel to buy Wisconsin!

His voice was by turns combative and wheedling, yet simmering with leadership and vision.

— I'm out there gettin' beat up for you, an' youse guys treat *me* like *dis*? he asked, offended, as if the steelworkers were three-time losers, freeloaders, ingrates or worse, who were impugning his sterling reputation.

— I was always dere for you, and now you, *you* don't trust *me*? he asked, a tremolo giving wing to his voice, and tears shimmering in his eyes.

Bobby B had discovered the Philosopher's Stone and wielded its legendary powers to his advantage. He could now hammer the base and leaden emotions of anger and mistrust and hatred into hope, golden and malleable hope.

— I bet Wisconsin'll be up 'n' runnin' soon, Bobby B triumphantly declared, stabbing his constituents in the heart with the sharpest point of the hope he had just fashioned.

After a moment of stunned silence and disbelief, the steelworkers burst into cheers. The bodyguards hustled Bobby B away through the agitated crowd into the dark refuge of his limousine, which spirited him away to his lawyerly redoubt. The temporarily pacified steelworkers, praising their representative in City Hall, milled about in the raw wind and rehearsed the glittering high points of his speech.

— Bobby B's gonna to take care o' t'ings!

— You heard him say it was all smoke and mirrors!

— Bobby B's a hero!

— You heard what he said: *Wisconsin'll be up 'n' runnin' soon!*

— Bobby B's gonna stand up ta da greedy fuckin' businessmen and bankers and lawyers and two-bit politicians 'n' crack da fuckin' whip.

— Bobby B's a great hunky, a great Chicagoan, a great American!

The news crew was quick to take advantage of the crowd's keyed up emotions to get their hard luck stories as well as their hopes. Jessica and the cameraman milled through the crowd, interviewing anyone who would speak to them.

— The camera's on. Go right ahead, said Jessica.

— Wisconsin fucked me outta severance pay, benefits, and vacation pay. Dat's more 'n twenny grand, ranted Chubby Boy.

— Let's start over, asked Jessica. This time without the profanity, otherwise we can't use it.

Then Gino got his close-up.

— I'm forty-six years old and I was walkin' tall up until 1980. I had dignity. Now I'm just a bum. I don't want welfare. I wanna work. Nobody really cares dat people are losin' everyt'in' cuz da comp'ny stabbed us inna back. People are tryin' to sell deir houses fer ten cents onna dollar. Fam'lies are gettin' smashed up, goin' to pieces. Divorce.

The camera pulled back to reveal that his right arm had been amputated at the elbow.

— I swear to God, nobody really cares!

Javi, Take One:

— My family came from Mexico tryin' ta find a better life. I was born in Chicago. I started as labor 'n' worked my way up ta better jobs. When da mill shut down, I was a spark tester. I was all set ta get a better job, like a roll builder, assemblin' bearin's — you name it.

King Peter, Take Two:

— I told management they was gonna be hell to pay if they didn't repair them cranes. They was gonna go at any minute 'n' kill somebody. A red-hot scrap end can bounce right outta da bucket and hit some guy below and *boom!* — kill 'im.

Bronx, Take One:

— *Da plant's shut down. Don't bother comin' in tomorrow. Prolly never.* Dat's what da plant manager tol' me. I didn't believe it cuz da night before Wisconsin management called a big meetin' for alla workers ta t'ank 'em for *rescuin'* da comp'ny. Da government loaned Wisconsin Steel millions ta rebuild a blast furnace dat was ready to go. It wuz dangerous. So why was da plant shuttin' down?

Jane Crane, Take One:

— The shutdown made the lives of women of Wisconsin Steel families real tough. Some families had no money saved up, so feedin' the kids got to be a problem. And havin' medical insurance cut off just like that. What happens if my husband or kid gets sick or hurt? And then I don't understand how the government owns the plant now. Why don't they put people back to work instead of makin' 'em collect welfare? And what're the kids gonna do? Join gangs?

Gavin, Take Two:

— Is it da workin' people's fault? No way, Jose. American corporations are up and takin' their factories to starvin' countries and turnin' 'em into wage slaves for fi'teen-twenty cents an hour. They don't want no Americans to be makin' thangs cuz they pocket more money with slave labor. That's why we're in such bad shape. American comp'nies, they go to Mexico, Brazil, Philippines, and then those wage slaves over there sell those products right back to us here inna States, rammin' these scab products down the throat of the American peoples. The system ain't takin care of the little guy.

The icy wind bared its teeth and began to gnaw and numb the men's limbs. Darkness threatened to fall swiftly.

A lone voice cried in the distance.

> *What do we want?*
> *We want Justice!*

The men had to keep moving, moving, moving to stay warm, which led them to disperse like outnumbered freedom fighters who had skirmished to a draw against larger fascist forces. The excitement was over, so some kept moving on their way to nowhere, while others headed back to the Capri for a couple of quick ones before resuming their journey to nowhere.

Slanting bars of rain needled the steelworkers as they swung back past Loncar's Liquors, past the Polka Sausage Company, past the YMCA, past Dudek's Religious Goods, past the South Chicago Library, past Gassman's, past the Washington Hotel, where Mike stumbled and fell to one knee. He kept his sign up, but his trouser leg was wet. His cold and wet feet were freezing. He looked around for the cameraman to see if this embarrassing moment had been caught on film, but the cameraman was gone. The news van was gone too. Jim and Jessica, his new best friends, and the crew had left without even saying good-bye.

Jan Polski joined Bronx and Mike on the way back to the Capri. They had to walk with their hands in their pockets, inclined against a stiff and rainy head wind.

— You stood up to Bobby B, man! said Jan. What did George Washington say? That was inspired! The crowd loved it!

— Dat cocksucker still needs some tire iron therapy, replied Bronx.

Mike lost all patience and shoved his brother.

— I could fuckin' kill you!

— Hey, hey, settle down, cried Jan as he separated them like a referee.

— Whose fuckin' bright idea was it to threaten Bobby B, huh? raged Mike, jabbing his finger at Bronx.

— You never once fuckin' stood up for me! Not once! Your own brother!

— I wish you just woulda kept yer big fuckin' mouth shut, shot back Mike irritably. It was disrespectful and un-fucking-professional. You ruined everythin'. You're an embarrassment to the family.

— Fuck you, Mike. Why you standin' up for Bobby B? asked Bronx. He ain't gonna do jack shit fer you.

— He's right, said Jan, raising his eyebrows. You don't have to ratiocinate to figure that one out.

Mike was tongue-tied.

— What's the fuckin' use, Mike finally said with no little disgust and resignation. I just wanted da demonstration to be a success and not get on Bobby B's bad side and have his gorillas kill somebody cuz o' some stupid shit.

— Can we please have a drink like grown-ups? asked Jan.

Welcome warmth drove the cold out of their clothing as they re-entered the Capri. Gino had returned the coffin there on his sound truck. Then the pallbearers stowed it anticlimactically in one of the small rooms above the restaurant. No one wanted to see it around anymore. The coffin had served its purpose.

Mike splashed money on the counter. Louie was serving drinks. Frank came by to thank Mike, King Peter, Javi, and Jan for all of their hard work.

— Here's to our public relations victory, toasted Jan. And three cheers for Frank Lumpkin!

— No, it's all of you, said Frank, who graciously excused himself.

They lavished praise on Frank as they watched his solitary figure walking away past the window and into the rain and gathering night.

— You made a great speech, said Gavin, who noticed that Mike had become uncharacteristically glum.

— You're a natural talker and you brought back memories, said King Peter. And you got the TV news to come out.

They drank up, then Mike slammed his glass down forcefully on the bar.

— Whose smart idea was it to try and beat the fuck outa Bobby B?

The men were silent.

— That fucked everything up! he said. We need unity, not infightin'.

— He's a lyin' sack o' chit, said Javi, finally speaking up. I just felt like hurtin' him. It just kinda happened.

— It ain't like brainin' a scab, said Mike reproachfully. I ain't gonna tolerate no fuckin' violence. Besides, Bobby B's gorillas woulda put youse all in da hospital if dey didn't kill ya.

Javi lowered his eyes.

— Whadja think o' Bobby B's speech? Mike asked Jan in order to change the subject.

— Let me put it this way, chuckled Jan, *If you don't get the Polak joke, then maybe you're the Polak.*

— Huh? asked Mike.

No one knew what he was getting at.

— You let Bobby B upstage you and Joe and Frank.

Mike felt a chill.

— He's a better politician 'n I am. I can't do nuthin' 'bout dat.

— Yeah, countered Jan, but why did you let him speak in the first place? It was *your* demonstration. He showed up for ten minutes, took over, and left owning it.

— Cuz I didn't wanna be disrespectful. 'Sides, he was helpin' us get Karl Malden.

— And did Malden show?

Mike fell silent.

— Bobby B's the Councilman, elaborated Jan. He's the Alderman. He was attorney for the union, and he was attorney for Harvester, continued Jan, gesturing airily with his hands, teasing every bit of meaning out of his words.

— He's right inna thick of it. He's got his hands in all da pies, said Mike with begrudging respect.

— That's called *conflict of interest*, said Jan with devastating authority.

The words *conflict of interest* spiked in Mike's ear. To the best of his knowledge, no one ever did hard time for conflict of interest.

— Remember when Walter Jacobsen came out with his crusading exposé of union finances? Bobby B was accepting contributions from both the company and the union.

— Who gives a fuck about conflict of interest, as long as da conflict is goin' in our interest? said Mike, running easily with the turn of a phrase that he thought just might rescue him.

— He ain't lookin' out for you, said Jan, leaning forward to emphasize his point. Bobby B's got an ulterior motive: he's lookin' out for number one. It's unethical for a lawyer to be representing two opposing sides in a dispute. Strictly speaking, he could be disbarred for it.

Mike scowled to show his disapproval of the direction the conversation had taken.

— O, yeah! emphasized Jan, raising his eyebrows and suggesting that Mike was out of his depth.

— What does that really mean: disbarred?

— Here's what it means, Jan explained patiently. It means the bar association — the lawyers' union — punishes a bad lawyer by taking away his license to practice law. When the mill crashed, Bobby B shut down the union and walked. *I ain't got no beef against labor law*, he said. *But dere ain't no money in it.* So he left Tony holding the bag. Tony was just a working stiff who was in it way over his head. He couldn't figure out the Wall Street deal, and Bobby B wasn't gonna wise him up. And then Harvester asked Tony to sign a pension guarantee document, which sounded just hunky dory to Tony, who's no Einstein, so he signed it. He shit in his pants later when he found out that he had gotten Harvester off the hook for more than sixty million in pension liabilities. Then Tony disappears like one of those guys in your *Strange but True* book, said Jan, in an aside to Bronx. No one ever saw him again. He was the captain of the ship who had survived the shipwreck, but thousands of his passengers died, and their bodies are still washing up all over South Chicago.

— Who gives a fuck if dey say dat it's gonna be da biggest pension payout in history, said King Peter. Guys like me an' you who put in twenty-plus years in the mill ain't gettin' diddly squat.

— Who gives a fuck about contracts? replied Bronx with morbid merriment as he gestured to Louie for another beer.

— Dey do whatever da fuck dey wanna do cuz dey got money 'n' lawyers, said Javi. We'll be lucky to get ten cents onna dollar.

— My point is, resumed Jan, that like any crooked politician who's been cornered, Bobby B had to make you believe in his bullshit for fifteen minutes, just long enough to give you hope, just long enough to get the fuck out of here without getting his ass kicked. Why do you think he had all those body guards to begin with? They were packin' heat, too. Bobby B was scared shit. The steelworkers are goin' down, and he's hopin' that after today's demonstration, you guys will run out of gas, roll over, and drop dead, so you'll never be able to assemble in such numbers and challenge his authority again. The rugged individualism of the old days up and died. Nowadays, rugged individualism is scabbism. America is set up that way. Cross that fuckin' picket line, man. Cut your own deal.

Mike, Bronx, King Peter, Javi and Gavin were stunned by Jan's pessimism.

— You think South Chicago was set up to make steel because of the lake and canal and docks? asked Jan in a new aggressive tone fueled by alcohol. Let me give you a lesson from labor history. In 1893, Eugene Debbs led a strike against Pullman. The government smashed the strike and dumped Debbs in the shitter like he was leading a guerilla uprising. Then guess what happened. The government built Ft. Sheridan so that U.S. Army troops could bust any Chicago strike, because US 41 leads right here. And then they built the Great Lakes Naval Station so they could send lake boats armed with big-ass guns down here at the drop of a hat to arbitrate disputes.

— Whose side are you on? asked Bronx.

Jan pursed his lips and shook his head.

— I'm tellin' ya what you're up against.

— It doesn't surprise me, said King Peter with thoughtful resignation. Tito was the same. But we thought this was the land of the free an'—

— I don' wan' no fuckin' settlement, said Gino, stepping back and looking at his shoes. No way.

— But say you get twenny thousand dollars? asked Mike, trying to stand up for Gino after Gino stopped standing up for himself.

— Look, Gino said, snickering nastily. Fuck da settlement. I don' wan' it. It's just fuckin' trouble for me if I get it. I donwanna get booted offa welfare. After all dey did to me, fuck 'em. I got disability. I got welfare. Fuck 'em.

— Right now, somewhere on the North Side, people are expressing their humanitarian ideals by holding wine and cheese party fundraisers to save whales and baby seals, Sandanistas and Vietnamese boat people, California redwoods and Pacific Northwest salmon, opined Jan. But nothing for steelworkers. We're the wrong kind of cause.

The rest of the city viewed South Chicago as semi-detached from the city proper, an area inhabited by working-class Morlocks, where brute force ruled brutes. On a clear night, when cold Canadian air blasted a hole in the sulfurous air, one could see headlights streaming past on the Skyway. For nearly twenty years, the Skyway permitted Northsiders to go straight to the Indiana Dunes and parts still farther east while bypassing the neighborhood, which was now hidden, locked in a closet like a retarded child to be secretly starved to death and buried in the backyard under the cloak of midnight.

All things draw the onset of the future, which is now unreal, but which must at some precise moment materialize.

— We seen de age of steel come 'n' we seen it go, said Bronx in response to Jan's grim appraisal, and it too sounded like the beginning of a speech, but the last vowel frisbeed away because Bronx had no other words to follow.

— Da kids figured it out. Dat first Christmas was da first time dey didn't get nuthin' dey wanted, said Mike. Or dey'd see some shit on TV, like a Cabbage Patch Doll or a BMX bike, and dey'd ask: *Why can't we get stuff like other kids get?* And you know damn well dere was no way I could buy it for 'em.

Mike, however, shook off his growing pessimism and ordered a round of drinks.

— When da Harvester board of directors sees da news, dey're gonna shit in deir pants, said Mike confidently, looking up to the television with vivid anticipation.

Louie served the next round.

— Here's to the settlement! said Mike.

The men drank up.

— Yeah, said Gavin. The settlement.

There was a pause in the conversation as the men watched the TV, where they sought distraction from their own private dilemmas.

King Peter, who had been sitting in skeptical silence, finally piped up:

— How are your kids, Mike?

Mike slid back onto his barstool. His eyes misted over.

— Dat bitch, said Mike, ostensibly referring to his ex-wife, didn't even bring da kids ta da demonstration. Maybe dey'll see it on TV. Maybe kids at school'll go, *Hey, I saw your ol' man on TV!*

Mike took a swig of his beer, then wiped his mouth with his back of his hand.

— We usta have arguments when we didn't have things. After da shutdown, sometimes I'd be under a lotta pressure cuz I was always da perviver. I'd feel like I couldn't cut the mustard. I usta have responsibility. I was a man. *I'm bringing home de bacon — and what I sez goes* 'n' alla dat shit. It tore me apart. It tore apart most other guys.

Mike was silent for a long time. Then his head began to sway as if he were listening to a song on a jukebox.

— So dat's where all the fuckin' money went, said Bronx, swiveling onto the barstool next to Jan.

— Yep, replied Jan. Harvester's attorneys took the title to the Great Lakes ore fields away from Envirodyne.

— What does that mean?

— It's like repossessing your home after you default on mortgage payments. The mill got zero fuckin' assets now, because the ore fields were the only real asset they had, elaborated Jan, taking an angry swig, then setting down the beer bottle on the bar where he turned it idly. It took a long, long time to figure out that Wisconsin's management and its board of directors had criminally conspired to strip the workers of their health and pensions benefits.

— Barbeque! shouted Bronx when he saw Darius walk by.

— Barbeque! replied Darius, and they shook hands.

— Where da fuck did eighty fuckin' million dollars in the pension fund go? asked Javi.

— Dose fuckers dey just robbed it, said King Peter.

— See? In 1979, Harvester forced the union at its farm equipment and truck plants — Wisconsin's biggest customers, mind you — out on strike, continued Jan. So, Wisconsin Steel couldn't make its mortgage payments to Harvester after it lost those orders. Then Harvester, the master manipulator —

Jan and Mike stopped to watch the expression on Bronx' face when he learned from Darius about what happened to Fred. Then they drifted into another conversation.

— Darius sez Fred got shot to death in some school yard, said Bronx, struggling thigh to thigh with a new phantom. I was kinda hopin' to see 'im.

— You kicked his ass but good, but you didn't move in for de kill, said King Peter.

— You zigged when you shoulda zagged, said Jan.

— Dat's cause I was fightin' old me, said Bronx with lateblooming wisdom. My reputation was shit cuz everyone knew dat I sent dose four guys to clean dat blast furnace... you know? Fred was fuckin' around.

— Uncle Sam's got to step in, said Mike, letting his head hang low over his boilermaker. *Yankee Doodle do or die.*

The rising effervescent bubbles in the throat of his glass of beer hypnotized Mike. I spent years hustlin' to bring respected Black roll hands into the union. I played softball, threw picnics, and Christmas parties. And firin' Fred woulda got 'em pissed off. Dey woulda turned deir back on me and Gavin. All woulda been lost. Either I fucked over the union or I fucked over Bronx. Hunkies thought I was a niggerlover. My brother sez I stabbed 'im in de back. Dat's why he fucked with Bobby B, just to stick it to me. Now all is lost.

— Hey, what ever happened to Karl Malden? asked Bronx.

Mike reacted with mild annoyance and waved his hand dismissively.

— Karl Malden.... I don't know what happened, answered Mike, shaking his head slowly. He never showed. You know, after all de excitement wit' da demonstration and da speeches and Bobby B's bodyguards, I just fergot about him. Anyways, you can never tell wi' dese movie stars. Dey say one thing, and den dey go doin' another.

— We really didn't need him, said Gavin. We got da word out. We got on TV.

King Peter and Jan looked at one another conspiratorially.

— You wanna tell him? asked Jan. Mike should know about it.

A moue crossed Jan's lips, and he glanced down at his beer, took courage, and lifted his eyes to meet Mike's.

— Tell me what? asked Mike, his throat tightening, plucking a note of suspense from his voice.

— I'll tell you what happened, said King Peter. Karl Malden was never gonna show. That *Skagska* TV program was nuthin' but trouble for 'im.

— I don't get it, said Mike.

— Here's how. My neighbor, Steve, and his *kum* from Gary, dis guy named Rod, were visitin' me a coupla nights ago. Rod knows all about it. He sez Malden always wanted to do some movie with Serbs. So, when he finally got the deal to make *Skagska*, he wanted to shoot it in Gary, and he wanned to get the blessing of the priest, so he goes to this DP priest out there and asks him: Оче, благослови наш рад, and he gives this parish priest a copy of the screenplay to bless. The next day this priest, he gives Malden his blessing. Malden shoots the film and when it gets on TV, the priest from Gary shits in his pants. The first episode was about Skagska's daughter bein' addicted to Quaaludes. This dumb-ass priest gave Malden his blessing wit'out even readin' da screenplay, because he couldn't read English to begin with! He was fresh off da boat. So, dis priest don't even talk to Malden. Instead, to save face, he denounces Malden. He sez Malden's a bad Serb 'cause on his TV show he has a young Serb girl who's addicted to drugs and he sez Serbs don't use drugs, and Malden's ruinin' the reputation of the Serbian people, so they should throw him outa the church.

— I didn't know dat, said Mike, shaking his head in dismay.

— And dat ain't all. Dis priest gets da владика, you know, the bishop, to back him up! You see, we call dat српска посла. Now Malden don' wanna have nuthin' to do with Serbs. He had it up to here with Serbs. He got his hit TV program. He got his American Express commercials. Why should he give a fuck about us? We're our own worst goddamn enemies.

— It's just like da church split, said Bronx, lighting his cigarette with uncharacteristic thoughtfulness. One group of Serbs is stabbin' another group of Serbs in the back over sump'n' stupid.

— I ain't no Serb! Mike vehemently objected, because he felt pain, which he thought had been lulled, irritated once again. I'm an American! I always presented myself as an American labor leader, a Hunkie whose heritage just happened to be Serbian instead of bein' an Orthodox churchgoin' Serb. I was a role model for Blacks and Mexicans. If a Serb could make it, den dey could make it too. I took no sides onna Church split, and it paid off. I had da support of key allies on bot' sides in order to get reelected. I talk to Croats, the Serbs' worst enemies, and I talk to Polaks, Mexicans, Blacks — you fuckin' name it.... *Yaksi mash, chinga tu madre, va fan culo,* and *bempti* fuckin' *my-koo.*

— Dere's nuthin' wrong with bein' a Serb, said Jan. I'm a Polak. People who never met Poles tell Polak jokes. But now with John Paul II, things are starting to change. Just be patient. It'll change for Serbs, too. For the better.

— I don't think so, Mike shot back. Even though I'm a DP, I'm ashamed of bein' a Serb, a member of dat cursèd race. I'm sick and fuckin' tired of endless arguments between *Federalci* and *Razbojnici,* arguments about Tito versus Drazha Mihailovich, bad stuff Croats, Ustashe, Muslims, and dose strange devils whoever dey are, dem Shiptars, done to Serbs. Dat's all over with. You name it, 'n' Serbs got opinions. Well, I got my own opinions. I work wi' Croats. Dey're all right. It bugs me when I t'ink how only Serbs stand up for Drazha, when everybody else dumped 'im as a Nazi collaborator. And den da Serbs got deir own version of history dat no one else believes or much less cares about, not to fuckin' mention Kosovo and St. Sava and all dat other hooey.

Alcohol loosened the reins of Mike's tongue.

— I ain't got no time fer dese two-hour church services. I live in a buy-sell, work-play, fight-fuck, kiss-and-make-up world. God only shows his face when there's marryin', buryin', 'n' baptisms. I'm sick 'n' tired o' Serbs 'n' Serbian problems cuz I got All-American problems at home.

Mike's eyes flared.

— And, you know what? Da Serbs are ashamed o' me too! Dey said dat I sacrificed my fam'ly and faith to become an American. Dat I forgot who I was, and dat I only knew a coupla words o' Serbian. Dat I married an American woman who came from a Croat family. *But Joe Polak marries Italian 'n' nobody cares.* Serbs think I sold out — dat I'm some kind a *january* or whatever the fuck they call it. But I'm a modern American man! he cried, banging his drink on the table.

Mike was intimidated by the sound of his own voice when he realized that he was speaking louder than anyone else in the bar.

— Maybe it's better I don't say nuthin', said King Peter. But Chika Drazha wasn't no collaborator.

— Most people around here are happy the mill closed, said Javi. Dis neighbor she sez to me, *See what happens when you get greedy? See?* Dey was glad to see us take it onna chin. Dey was jealous. Now dey don' give a shit.

— Keep my seat warm, said Mike as he rose, responding to nature's call.

The cold air in the john braced Mike as he sidled up to a urinal next to Ivo Pivo.

— Great speech, Mike, said Ivo.

— Thanks!

— I appreciate you mentionin' my name, too, added Ivo. It'll gimme credibility when I start as precinct captain.

Mike suppressed a disagreeable spasm.

— Congratulations, said Mike, speaking softly to the wall with his eyes closed. When did you get the good news?

— Yesterday. Bobby B called me up and asked me to stop by the office. I was really surprised. I didn't t'ink I was gonna get it.

The spasm passed, but it left a trap door in its wake, through which Mike had begun to fall.

— I'm very happy for you, said Mike, withholding his aggrieved disappointment.

Mike closed his eyes again as he drained his bladder. Why did Bobby B give Ivo da job? After all I done. Why? And Ivo sez he found out yesterday, so da demonstration didn't mean jack shit. He played me for a —

— You know, Mike, now I can take care of my fam'ly, said Ivo earnestly. I wuz really hurtin' before.

Mike washed his hands at the sink, and then dried them with a stiff paper towel.

— You'll be an out*stan*din' precinct captain, said Mike like a real pro.

He laughed and shook Ivo's hand as he fell further through the trap door.

— I just wanna say, added Ivo, dat I don't pay no attention to dat Serb-Croat stuff. You wuz always fair. Workin' wit' you showed me how to talk to people and be a leader and —

— Let's get back in, said Mike abruptly. Da news is comin' on.

Mike surged through the bathroom door, leaving Ivo nonplussed.

— I'm tryin' to tell you somethin', Mike! Ivo called out with sudden urgency, but Mike was falling to his recently vacated barstool, and the people in the bar were falling with him, and the bar and the barstool and the outside world were falling with him.

Mike's dreamchildren were falling. A dreamblackbird cawed in the sky.

— Bobby B's an American, too, but he ain't ashamed to say he's a Croat, said Jan, picking up the thread of his thought. He ain't no Hunky. He made that up just to get Serbs and Polaks and Croats to vote for him so he doesn't have to say White people.

Mike's jaw tightened as he was falling, falling, falling.

— Everybody in South Chicago knows old man Brkljacha roasted a lamb the day the Ustashi killed King Aleksander in Marseille, added King Peter.

— If you get a flashlight, 'n' look up Bobby B's ass, you'll see he's Irish, just like Bilandic, said Mike obscurely.

— Listen, Bobby B couldn't get Malden to come out here anymore than you could, huffed Jan. He just got you to play up the rumor that Karl Malden was gonna come to get a good crowd to turn out for the demonstration so that he'd have the biggest possible audience to address. That's Bobby B for you!

Mike's face hounddoged, his jaw slackened, and his face went numb as the theme song for the news kicked in and rescued him from speechless shock. Louie turned up the sound.

The bar quickly fell silent and anyone could hear the cigarette smoke rising into the rafters. The lead story was about the Soviets pulling out of nuclear disarmament talks in Geneva; a Dunbar High School student beaten to death with a baseball bat; a shooting on the West Side; the Mayor opposed a real estate tax increase. Then commercials: Tidy Bowl with a calypso theme, featuring a White man in a yachtsman's outfit accompanied by a barefoot Black man in a beachcomber hat and cut-offs who was playing a guitar, were standing on a raft afloat in a toilet bowl. Then, *If I Could Teach the World to....*

— Shiyeet! Dey said we was gonna be on da news, complained Bronx in perfect harmony.

— World and national news come first, said Jan. Don't ask me why!

Television wasn't just *Johnny Carson*, *Love Boat*, and *Streets of San Francisco*. It could just as well relate powerful, true stories that turned public opinion against injustices as varied as the Viet Nam War, segregation, and Love Canal. All television had to do was present the plain facts of the death of steel in order to redress the injustice that the steelworkers had suffered. Why was that so hard to do?

After the station switched back to the news desk, the newscaster began the story about the Thanksgiving Eve demonstration in South Chicago. They cut to a two-second shot of South Chicago that the nameless cameraman had taken from the Skyway, the rich man's view of the neighborhood. The announcer's voice said something about a demonstration against the shutdown of Wisconsin Steel. Then they showed a three-second shot of Frank Lumpkin and Joe Francisco and Mike leading the demonstrators down Commercial Avenue with the coffin and pallbearers behind them. The scan lines sliced the image and destabilized it. Mike was alarmed by how small everything looked and how fleetingly he appeared on screen.

Television ain't big like movies, it hit Mike. TV's small, but more people see it right away.

Then they cut to three seconds of Joe Francisco shaking his head and saying, *It's terrible, it's terrible*, which gave Mike yet another vivid and disagreeable shock.

Cut to Frank Lumpkin, who spoke straight into the camera: *The lawyers are right on the case.*

Cut to Gino, shaking his head: *I don't want welfare. I wanna work.*

Cut to Javi, whose face was still wet with rain: *When da mill shut down, I wuz a spark tester.*

Cut to Jane Crane, who was wearing a red bandana to hold her hair in place: *The shutdown made the lives of the women of Wisconsin Steel families real tough.*

Cut to Gavin, who looked into the mic as he spoke: *The system ain't takin' care of the little guy.*

Then they cut to ten seconds of angry Bobby B in medium-close-up, talking a line of shit a yard wide and a mile long from the sound truck, and he ended with: *I bet Wisconsin'll be up 'n' runnin' soon!*

Cut to crowd shots of cheering steelworkers. Then cut back to the newscaster in the studio, who nodded gravely and then segued into sports.

That was all.

The news story made it appear as if Bobby B had done all the work to get the workers' jobs back instead of the Save the Steel Mills Committee. Jim had played Mike. They cut out everything else: the pre-demonstration gathering at the Capri, Mike's speech, Frank's speech, Bobby B's bodyguards, the rain bespattered demonstrators, the hard-luck stories. The news report had morphed into a commercial for Bobby B that upstaged the entire demonstration, along with Mike, who began the day as a major character, and was now ending it as an extra carrying an illegible sign in the rain. The neighborhood, its steel mills, and its workers had merely become art direction, scenery, and extras in an unreal teledrama.

The men sat slack jawed, paralyzed with disappointment.

— Dat's fuckin' bullshit, man! hollered Mike, surging from his barstool. Turn that fuckin' thing off, Louie!

Mike, sterilized by the news clip, slumped back on his barstool.

— You did da best you could, Mike.

— Yeah, at least we got on TV.

— We're fucked, man, said Mike, trying to rub the Anacin Headache #7 out of his temples.

Louie got the jukebox started to distract the men.

Mike was still falling, sinking now in an ocean of unfulfilled expectations. He was drowning, gasping for air as he was being dragged further down by a frigid undertow to depths where no sunlight ever reached, sinking all the way down to the hidden lair of old refrigerators, stolen cars, and nameless hoodlums garbed in concrete overcoats.

Mike kept falling until he fell into the gutted remains of Kompare's Funeral Home. Smokey shafts of sunlight pierced the ceiling; and he saw broken pieces of serbianna: headless wartime memorial statuary, pages torn from Cyrillic books scattered on the floor; a fire-stained Turkish coffee pot; torn lace doilies; chipped cut-crystal ashtrays; a heavily stained woven rug depicting Stefan Adamović's *Battle of Kosovo*; a half-burnt slava candle; dried herbs and mints; a winepress filled with dirty laundry; tattered copies of the *American Srbobran*; a pair of well-worn *opanke*; a torn bumper sticker that read *Niko nema što Srbin imade*; a shot glass bearing an insignia of four esses; a tangled *pojas*; half a pack of stale Drina cigarettes; a 78 record called *Arijevsko kolo* produced by Balkan Music Corporation; Geca Kon's *Bukvar*; and prominent amidst the rubble, there was a lectern bearing a tattered icon of Saint Sava. Enter Alfred Causey and Otis Jones, one with head wounds from a blunt object and the other whose head had been disfigured by a mallet; Hilding Anderson, Leo Francisco, Lee Tisdale, and Kenneth D. Wood, all suffering gunshot wounds to the chest; Anthony Tagliori and Joseph Rothmund with gunshot wounds to the stomach and neck, respectively; Earl Hundley and Sam Popovich whose faces were smashed in and half blown-off, all cut down Memorial Day on May 30, 1937, at the gates of Republic Steel.

— *We wuz paradin' for da right to organize a union*, says Lee Tisdale at the lectern. *To promote industrial democracy 'n' secure justice and equality fer workin' men and women everywhere....*

Bronx tossed back a shot.

— I wasn't carryin' no empty coffin, said Bronx with grim sincerity. Dat coffin was carryin' Wally Koza, Pedro Garcia, Jimmy Nolan, and Lazo Babich. Dey wuz here in spirit.

The light in the windows had dimmed to slate gray. The neon sign flashed blue, then red: *old eer.* Beyond, the lonesome railroad platform where no trains had stopped for twenty years.

— *It's three a.m.,* sang the jukebox with Sinatra's voice, padded by sustained piano chords.

The phantom singer, emphasized by his absence, caused Bronx to unwittingly suspend his disbelief and presume that phantom Frank Sinatra was addressing him personally, and even sat on the torn red vinyl upholstery of the adjacent bar stool.

— *If you could boss 'em around while they was alive and send 'em to clean out that blast furnace, then you gotta pay your respects to the dead,* said phantom Frank, urging Bronx to accept the way things are. *They was takin' orders from you.*

— Dat ain't what's eatin' me, Bronx told phantom Frank. Why did Mike fuck me over like dat? He stood up for Fred and Darius. My own brother stabbed me in de back.

— *Some cats just swing like that,* replied Frank.

Phantom Wally Koza bellied up to the bar.

— *Ya buyin', Bronx?*

— Wally, ya fucker! Have a shot on me!

Next came phantom Pedro Garcia and phantom Jimmy Nolan.

— We got room for everybody, said Bronx. Line 'em up, Louie!

— *How are my kids,* asked phantom Jimmy Nolan.

— Okay. They miss you beatin' their ass.

— *How's my wife?* asked phantom Pedro.

— She's still workin' at de A&P. Don' worry, I ain't jockin' her!

— *What happened to my '66 Mustang?* asked phantom Wally.

— Some Polak in Hegewish bought it and smashed it up on de S-curve.

Phantom Lazo was just staring at Bronx, so Bronx initiated a conversation with him to dispel his discomfort.

— I'm sorry I sent you guys to clean out dat blast furnace. A day don't go by widout me thinkin' 'bout it. Well, I guess yous guys come fer me, so it must be that time.

— Нисмо дошли за тебе. Дошли смо за другога, said Lazo.

Bronx picked up his glass. Phantom Sinatra picked up his.

We're drinking my friend, to the end....

Jan elbowed Bronx and said:

— Remember when Tito joined the choir? And I came over and brought you a twelve pack! You said *Tito's really fuckin' dead? I wish I could go to the funeral and piss on his grave!*

— Huh? asked Bronx, blinking with astonishment. I 'member sayin' that.

— Now when Gomulka kicks the bucket, you gotta get me a twelve pack, okay?

— Tito's dead, said Bronx, unsure of what Jan was getting at. Yeah, I'll get you a twelve pack.

— Some analysts are saying Yugoslavia's gonna fall apart, continued Jan. And Ivo says Croatia's gonna be independent one day. Any comment?

— Croats, said King Peter. They was independent when they was Nazis in WWII. Besides, I don't think they're gonna get the U.S. on their side if they keep on settin' off bombs inna Statue of Liberty. But there are good Croats too.

— Why did the U.S. drop its support for Mihailovich in the middle of the war and switch to Tito? asked Jan. Nobody can answer that one.

— King Peter could tell ya, said Bronx. Ain't dat so, Mike? and then he noticed that Mike was gone.

— Where da fuck did Mike go? I ain't finished wit' 'im yet. I'm gonna take him to Estrella's to have his dick straightened out after I bust his balls a little more.

The guys tittered. No one knew what to say next in the themeless moment.

— Tell Jan why America dumped Mihailovich during WWII, Bronx said to King Peter.

— The real King Peter was a loyal ally of the U.S. who was betrayed by English Communists in MI5. It was a Communist plot, and Mihailovich —

— Communist plot! Ha ha ha! laughed Jan scornfully, setting the guys at the bar on a laughing jag.

— I'm serious, said King Peter.

— *Comrade Boobinski, what happened?* Everything can be explained by a Communist plot, said Jan, wiping tears of laughter from his eyes.

King Peter's eyes misted over.

— Serves me right for mentionin' a great man's name in a —

Then King Peter noticed that Bronx wasn't laughing, but coughing up bloody spittle into a paper napkin.

— You alright? inquired King Peter, slapping Bronx' back.

— I went to da VA Hospital for a checkup last week. Dey tol' me I ain't got middle-aged acne. Dey diagnosed it as chloracne. Da bleedin' in my mouth and gums dey t'ink is multiple myeloma.

— What da fuck's that?

— Fuck if I know. I was afraid t'ask, he said, folding the napkin which he secreted in his pocket. I gotta go back next week. You know, I ain't been da same since dat fight.

Bronx lit another cigarette and urgently took a drag. His mouth left the filter tip pink with blood.

— Why didn't Mike stand up for you? asked Javi.

Silent veins of anger darkened Bronx' neck.

— I didn' take it personal cuz Mike is fucked up, said Bronx. He did what he did cuz o' union politics.

— I know he got divorced, said King Peter. Him 'n' Eileen usta be so happy. What happened?

Bronx felt sufficiently fortified to speak.

— Mike met Eileen in high school, said Bronx. Everybody knew dat her ol' man, Bill Starcevich, died when she was still a kid. Mike stepped in and filled da slot. I 'member goin' over dere and seein' dis pitcher o' de ol' man wearing a suit and smilin', hauntin' da front room. One day a coupla years ago, Mike tol' me Eileen comes home and she looks like she seen a ghost, not no fuckin' Caspar the friendly ghost either but a real fuckin' ghost. *I saw this man on Commercial Avenue who was the splittin' image of my dead father*, she sez. *Oh, yeah?* sez Mike. *I stopped him and said, 'Excuse me, but you look just like Bill Starcevich.'* And? *'I am Bill Starcevich'*, sez dis guy. *He was just lookin' at me wonderin' who I was. He didn't even recognize me.* Dat's what Eileen sez. *Is he da same guy or is he anudder Bill Starcevich? He could be pullin' yer leg*, goes Mike. *For Chrissake*, sez Eileen gettin' pissed off, *he's been livin' in da Washington Hotel, on 92nd and Commercial fer alla dese years. Dat's only a mile 'n' a half away. What da fuck wuz he doin dere alla dose years?* sez Mike, like his life is turnin' into a *Twilight Zone* episode. It's a lot easier fer a farmer ta walk inna his field one day and fuckin' disappear than to have this same farmer walk back inna his field twenny fuckin' years later, knockin' on da door, sayin' *Guess who's comin' ta dinner*? *Sump'n tells me dis guy's a con artist*, sez Mike. And Eileen is standin' up fer dis bum. *I'm gonna to take 'im out ta dinner ta da* Steak House, sez Eileen. *He really is my father. He 'members things we did.*

— That's strange, said King Peter, engrossed by the disclosure of Mike's heretofore untold hard luck story.

— Mike could tell from da way she said things dat she knew more 'n' she was lettin' on, said Bronx, watering his throat with beer. Dis means trouble, cuz wherever dere's some mystery, dere's bound to be fuckin' trouble. De ol' man, Mike figured, was prolly a gambler or a drunk or a drug addict or a con artist or maybe alla dem rolled up inna one big douche bag, and dat he wuz looking fer a hand-out, tuggin' Eileen's heart strings for a little moolah. But why didn't he ever call Eileen alla dem years? And why da fuck was he livin' only a mile 'n' a half away!?

Bronx looked around for Mike who was nowhere to be found.

— Where'd dat fuckin' bum go? he rhetorically asked.

King Peter, Javi, and Jan chuckled.

— Now you know why he stumbled in fronna da Washington Hotel. He was thinkin' about dat, said Bronx, spinning his index finger illustratively around his temple. He's fuckin' mental cuz o' dis. So Eileen takes dis guy out ta dinner, and comes back. *So is dis guy really yer ol' man?* sez Mike. *He really is my father*, she sez. *So where's he been?* sez Mike. *He had to make a fateful choice between his family 'n' love greater 'n his family.* Dat's how she put it, prolly repeatin' what he fuckin' told her. *An' what kinda love is dat?* goes Mike, suspectin' de old bastard had turned hippie or sump'n'. *It's not ordinary love, but spiritual love*, Eileen sez, you know, her voice ridin' kinda wobbly on dem tears she's holdin' back. *So what's he been doin' alla dis time?* goes Mike, starin' at her. *He was in love wid a bride of Christ*, Eileen sez to him. *A what?* goes Mike. *A bride of Christ*, she sez, waitin' fer it to sink in. *He some kinda holy roller or sump'n'?* goes Mike. *Not a holy roller, Mike. Spiritual*, she sez, gettin' all pissed off. *You always bring things down to the lowest common denominator.* An' Mike goes: *What the fuck is a bride of Christ?* cuz now he really wants to know and she's fuckin' holdin' 'im in suspense. Mike can't figure it out and Eileen still won't tell 'im straight. *I don't get it,* sez Mike. Finally, she sez *A priest. A Roman Cath—* ... Mike can't believe he's hearin' dis shit. *You're ol' man's been boffin' a Roman Cat'lic priest fer twenny years?* he sez. Eileen don't say a fuckin' thing. *He's my father, Mike,* said Bronx, cruelly imitating his former sister-in-law's strident voice for comic effect. *He can help out by takin' care o' da kids! Den I can go back ta work.*

Bronx slapped his thigh, and the others laughed out loud.

— *He can help out by takin' care o' da kids!* repeated Bronx for effect as his audience laughed even harder. Ain't dat a kick in de ass!

Bronx paused to pound down his beer. Suspense gripped his audience. Then Bronx, refreshed, continued:

— Mike blows 'is top: *I don't want dat cocksucker anywhere near my kids!* She goes, *He's their grandfather, for Crissake!* in dat screechy voice o' hers. *An' dey're my kids, too! A bride of fuckin' Jesus Christ? Jesus fuckin' Christ wasn't no homo!* sez Mike. Den Mike goes off on her: *Forgive me, Father, for I have sinned,* sez Mike in a femmy voice. *I sucked Father Flynn's cock before mass. O,* says the Bishop, *go say ten Our Fathers and ten Hail Marys. Dat's fuckin' sick! Serbs don' do dat shit.* Dat's what Mike sez. *You Cat'lics, you t'ink you can get away with anything, and den you confess, and den everything's okay like nuthin' happened. But it ain't okay. We raise our kids Serbian from now on. None of dis fuckin' Pope of Rome bullshit! I don't want no fuckin' queer in my house, even if he is your ol' man!*

— I met a lot of women, women friends, relatives, said Javi, introducing a moderating tone, and I know they're more stable than guys. In Mexico, men got this *macho* feeling. *Macho* means a guy can do whatever the fuck he wants to, and his wife can't do a damn thing about it. If Mike 'a gave 'im a break, maybe he'd still be married now.

— How do you know he'd keep it in his pants? asked Bronx. Would you trust him alone wit' da kids?

— Dat's not Mike's call. Dat's Eileen's call, said Javi. I think women are equal. You gotta learn how to respect women. She wanted her dad around. It's natural.

— And what if Eileen makes a bad call? asked Bronx. Businessmen, lawyers, engineers, politicians, dey all fuck up too, don't they? Ain't dat why we come out here for today?

Javi was about to develop his ideas further when Rico the scarfer came over and said something confidentially to Javi in Spanish. Javi rose quickly.

— See you guys later, said Javi over his shoulder, as he left. Gotta go!

Javi's comment about respect for women lingered in the air, then vanished like perfume.

— I remember your *slava*, said King Peter to Bronx.

It was nearly impossible to plan family activities or celebrate traditional family feast days because shift work kept everybody off balance. No one ever went to bed at the same time more than five times a week. Everyone was sleep deprived, and alternately angry or docile.

— I 'member you answered da door with your right eye still all purple and swollen shut. Den me and my wife sat down onna couch in your front room. Father Dragiša was packing up his cross and chalice and censer and the *slava* candle was burnin' on the table. Den Mike comes by wit' his kids. I shake hands wit 'im and your nephews an' niece. *Couldn't Eileen make it?* asks my wife. *Nah, she's busy*, sez Mike, kinda uncomfortable. *Her father an' stuff.* Den Mike said dat he wasn't sure how to explain to da kids what da *koljivo*, da *kolač*, and da *slava* candle all mean, why we celebrate it at home insteada church, so he asked Father Dragiša to tell da kids. But Father Dragiša don't speak English so good and da kids don' understand Serbian, so I 'splained dat da *krsna slava* celebrates da day when deir ancestors wuz baptized. Only da Serbian people celebrate da *slava*. I tol' 'em our ancestors accepted Christianity, but dey wouldn' give up the *slava* for nuthin', cuz they been celebratin' it for thousands o' years even before they wuz Christian. And you know how kids always tell da truth. Dey say what deir parents 'n' teachers tell 'em ta say. Pete, the oldest, goes *Father Bjazić* (that Croatian priest from the Cat'lic school) *says* slavas *are backwards and pagan.* Nobody said nuthin', and Mike started actin' like he didn't believe in any o' dat stuff anyway. He wuz so glad he was raisin' his family American. He was proud o' da kids goin' to Cat'lic school where dey was gonna get a good education. *For crissake, he sez, even high-class Serbs send deir kids dere. As long as da kids learn da Ten Commandments, everything'll be okay,* sez Mike. *Da past is all over with, all washed up.* So I sez *Is dat what you call an education?*

King Peter paused to scratch his temple thoughtfully with his middle finger, then drank again.

— That's how we lose 'em, said King Peter, gurning his jaw as he savored the brandy.

Gavin had been regarding these men with some apprehension and mistrustfulness. These guys were the sons of men — or in fact the same men — who had once tried to burn him out of his home in Trumbull Park. Even so, he found Mike's story strange and involving.

Back in the 1950s, the Trumbull Park Homes always had a bad reputation, and had been nicknamed "the red light district" because slutty single mothers allegedly lived there. People looked down on the place even before some Black families moved in, which triggered the longest period of rioting that Chicago had ever known. Blacks were jumped and beaten. Hooligans hurled Molotov cocktails at Black houses. When the cops showed up, they said, *Youse people can always move.*

— I had no idea Mike had those kinda problems. After you had dat fight wit' Fred, I had to make a show of standin' up for that lyin'-ass nigguh. I 'member I slammed da door in Mike's office and walked right up to his desk. I 'member his eyes. Dey were lookin' sad they way a hound dog do, the look a man gets when he got problems at home. *It's too much, man,* I say. *It's a thankless motherfuckin' job. Gavin,* sez Mike *I made sacrifices, too. No matter what I do,* I said, *some muthufuckuh ends up hatin' my fuckin' guts. I'm gonna continue supportin' you, Mike, but you gonna to have to find another assistant for your turn.*

Gavin sighed and rolled his eyes along the Capri's dark ceiling, then continued his tale:

— I jus' couldn' take it no more. I'll never give another comp'ny what I gave Wisconsin. I'll try my damndest, don' get me wrong. But if I can get away with anything, I do it. I don' give a fuck about no comp'ny no more. They made me feel this way. But I'll always respect Mike for teachin' me how to organize and get people together. I helped Gus Savage get elected to Congress, thanks t' what I learned from Mike. Anyway, I had no idea he was goin' through this shit. He musta been burnin' up inside.

— Where *is* Mike? asked Bronx impatiently. He turned and scoped the bar for the irascible grievanceman, who was nowhere to be seen.

— Hey, Louie, you seen Mike?

Louie wrinkled his forehead.

— Wasn't he just wichoo?

Bronx let his eyes slowly arc around the bar again, but Mike was not there.

— Like dat fucker just stepped off de face of de earth. Come on, said Bronx to the others, let's fuckin' go!

It was a frosty autumn night. The rain puddles on the street were freezing into patches of black ice. The sodium vapor lamps burned with an orange tinge that glinted off the gritty asphalt as King Peter, Bronx, Jan, and Gavin made their way to Estrella's, which occupied a three-story wooden A-frame with grimy asbestos siding.

Jan was holding forth his book learning.

— So, by the seventies, he said, union busting was gaining momentum. Guys were getting fired left and right, and unions couldn't fight back. Taft-Hartley seemed like a law of physics, but the old union guys fought like hell against it. Now I understand why.

— Why wuz they against it? asked Gavin.

— I used to smile smugly, thinking, *O, how immature!* It took me years to realize that Taft-Harly was a poison chalice: it *was* that fuckin' law after all. The poison didn't kill you right away. No, it was gonna kill you a little bit at a time over time. Guys who were born after Taft-Hartley learned that they were born with a fatal birth defect, so their days were numbered. Boy, I can can hear Taft and Hartley rollin' over in their graves. Joke's on you, fellas!

— You learned alla dis in law school, Jan? asked Bronx.

— Some.

— Why'd you go to law school out there insteada here?

— I took a map of the United States and a compass. I measured out five hundred miles on the legend. Then I put the needle on Chicago and drew a circle. So, I applied to any law school that lay outside —

The sharp sounds of a commotion in front of Estrella's interrupted the gang of four. A crazy Mexican was pounding on the door. A couple of other Mexicans were backing him up. The crazy Mexican kicked the door:

— *Donde esta mia muher!* he shouted at the windows upstairs. Then he paused for an answer, and when none was forthcoming, he tried to kick the door down again.

The Mexicans were too preoccupied with their assault on Estrella's to notice Bronx and the others across the street.

— Fuck, said Bronx with keen disappointment.

— *Donde esta mia muher!* the crazy Mexican yelled again with bloodcurdling fury.

He paused, then laid siege to the great dark door once again.

— Looks like amigo found out something dat he shouldn't have found out, said King Peter.

Jan read the emerging scene like a book, then his expression became downright funereal.

— That ain't some poor amigo. *That's Javi,* emphasized Jan.

— Let's get outa here before he sees us, urged Bronx.

— He better not see us here, said Gavin.

A blue and white flashing its blue light pulled up, but Javi did not relent. His companions fled. Two policemen emerged from the squadrol and subdued him quickly by knocking him to the ground, rolling him over on his stomach, and handcuffing his hands behind his back.

Bronx, Jan, Gavin, and King Peter withdrew past Heine's toward the 92nd Street Bridge to avoid any trouble. By the time they passed under the bright lights of the Sunoco station, they felt safe.

— Isabelle, that's her name, said King Peter. That's his wife's name.

As the wind picked up, Bronx zipped up his army surplus jacket. A half-moon peered over the high wind that still smelled of coke and ash. The men stood on the bridge besides which a mountain of rock salt, covered with tarpaulin and anchored by a network of rope and automobile tires, rose like a lump of nightmare in the earth's throat.

They stepped idly in pools of sodium vapor light, the poor man's spotlight.

— Juanita, Roselle, Cookie, Estrella, Isabelle — they're all gonna be there tomorrow, said Bronx.

— Maybe not Isabelle. I feel sorry for Javi, said King Peter.

— I know Isabelle, said Bronx.

— I was wonderin' why she didn't come ta da demonstration, said Gavin. She always usta come ta Union meetings wit' Javi.

— She the one wid de long black hair 'n' built like a brick shithouse?

— That be her, said Gavin.

— Shiyeet, said Jan.

— Javi better go easy on 'er, said King Peter. She's feedin' de fam'ly and payin' da bills now.

— I know what Javi's goin' through, said Bronx, taking account of the discomfort they felt. He's gonna hafta go ta marriage counselin'. Mike had ta go to fuckin' *marriage counselin'*.

The wind gusted. Bronx lit up. He passed the pack around. None of them wanted to resume their journey, but it was time to go on.

— I'll find somethin' soon, said Gavin, feeling horny and sad. I will. I ain't givin' up. That's what happens to a lotta people. They be givin' up. They don't keep lookin'. If you don't keep lookin', a job ain't gonna come ta you. Sure, sometimes ya get depressed. You don' wanna be goin' out an' lookin' no more. But ... fuck it.

— Twelve dollars an hour, eight dollars an hour, four dollars an hour. What's the difference? asked King Peter.

— Shiyeet, said Gavin.

— Computers, said Jan. That's gonna be the next big thing.

— Huh? asked Bronx.

— There's computer work out there now, said Jan, trying to give the guys a tip. You just need to learn how to type.

— You mean bein' a button pusher? asked Gavin.

— Then you have to learn a program or two..., continued Jan irresolutely.

A torrent of uproarious laughter surged from the steelworkers' throats, spiked here and there by guffaws, runaway mouth and nose laughter that snorted to a halt, then rose to arpeggios of peaking hahas, arching howls, and then subsided to desperate gasps for air to breathe again to laugh again to breathe again.

— I guess I better go back ta da Capri 'n' help Mike bring dat coffin back to Kompare's, said Bronx after he caught his breath. A fucking button pusher.

Jan, King Peter, and Gavin offered to help, so they trudged back to the restaurant.

The coffin was upstairs in a horrible little room where Save the Steel Mills had met. It had a low ceiling and the lights were always going out. The coffin seemed more powerful than before, unvanquished and fateful. It rested on a drop-leg table in the middle of the room. The wet American flag lay ingloriously on the floor, and it imparted the impression of a violated court of justice where Justice remained obstinately present.

— I fuckin' hate what they're doin' to us, said Bronx as he picked up the flag and draped it over a couple of folding chairs to dry. Dey're actin' like dey can get away wid anything. Maybe dere'll be a lawsuit, but de lawyers'll drag it out in court for twenny years till everybody — us, da judges, and da lawyers — are all fuckin' dead! Den dey'll settle. I jus' want blood now, man. Uncle Sam said *go to 'Nam* and I went. Den Wisconsin sez *do dis fucked up job*, so I did it. I thought this was America's way of sayin' *thanks*. I thought America guaranteed da whole fuckin' thing. I ain't even forty, but I'm all fucked up with boils on my ass and spittin' blood cuz I went to 'Nam 'n' den went to Wisconsin. I'm goin' to pieces, and ain't no woman gonna fuck me if I don't pay her cuz I'm inna fucked up situation. And look at how Big Business is payin' us back! It's fuckin' fucked up beyond belief! You know what de American Dream is? It's *Hurray for me and fuck you, pal.* Rob, steal, rip off as much as you can and fuck integrity. Dat went out wit' John Wayne and Crazy Horse. And you know what? Crazy Horse wuz fuckin' right. *White man speak with forked tongue.* And dat's just da way it is. Sky King and Penny can't help, GI Joe and Jane can't help, and Superman flyin' with Wonder Woman pullin' can't help. Right now, if dere wuz anudder war, you'd be fightin' for da rich. What dey did to us is a fuckin' sin.

King Peter, Jan, and Gavin were standing around the coffin, waiting for Bronx to finish his rant.

— Aw, fuck it, said Bronx. I'm sorry I ruined yer Charlie Brown Thanksgiving.

The secret city had secret streets and the secret streets had secret buildings, but there was no road map to this real world within the real world.

— Fuck Thanksgivin', said Bronx, now a broken-faced gargoyle of prehistoric rage. They shoulda put me in that fuckin' coffin.

Bronx grabbed one of the handles, Jan the other; Gavin the front and King Peter opposite him.

— One anda two anda —

Their limber arms, now accustomed to the weight of the oblong box, lifted, but it balked weightily. The men let the coffin drop as if they had been jolted by a live current. The drop-leg table shuddered beneath.

— Something's wrong here, muttered Jan, his voice splintering like a taut steel cable. It's not supposed to be this heavy.